CLARK SELBY

BOOK SIX

DANGEROUS ALLY

Library of Congress Control Number: 2025902862

ISBN
979-8-89641-040-9 (Paperback)
979-8-89641-041-6 (eBook)
979-8-89641-039-3 (Hardcover)

Dedication

This Book is dedicated to my wife, Karen Serene Selby for helping me with my books and to my two sons and their wives, Michael and Phyllis Selby and Robert and Janell Selby.

Table of Contents

C H A P T E R   O N E

CALL FROM THE PRESIDENT OF THE UNITED STATES

The telephone was ringing in Tom and Jenny's Beverly Hills mansion at six am on Sunday morning. It took a few minutes before the butler, Robert, answered the phone and said, "General and Mrs. Parker's residence."

A woman said, "This is a call from the President of the United States and he needs to speak with General Parker right away, please."

Robert replied, "Just a moment and I will see if I can get General Parker on the line for you, please hold."

Robert went to the door of Tom and Jenny's bedroom and knocked on the door. Then he heard Tom say, "Just a moment, Robert. I'll be right there."

Tom quickly put on his robe and went to the bedroom door, opened it and asked, "Is there a problem, Robert?"

"I don't know, sir, but the President's office is on the phone asking for you."

"Thank you, Robert. I'll get it."

Tom went over to a desk in the bedroom and picked up the phone and said, "This is Tom Parker."

The lady on the phone said, "Sir, just a moment for the President."

The President said, "General Parker. I'm sorry to bother you so early on a Sunday Morning, but I'm afraid I need your help."

Tom replied, "No problem, sir, what can I do to help you?"

"I need you to check up on someone who is supposed to be a strong ally of ours, but we're concerned he might be using us for his own personal benefit."

"All right, sir, who is this person?"

"His name is Blake Pearson, the Prime Minster of the United Kingdom ."

"Sir, are you sure you have a reason for thinking this? I'm sorry, but I have to ask, Mr. President, what makes you think he has changed sides?"

"Reports that I am getting from the Embassy; they are telling me that a Russian business man, Peter Valkovich, has been courting him and his wife with trips to Paris, and then to Moscow to attend the ballet.

"Apparently, Mr. Pearson's wife, Suri was an quite a ballerina before she was injured and could no longer perform. "

"Mr. President, do you have anything else to question his loyalty to us, besides this?"

"Well, our Ambassador, Steve Jones, says that he thinks there's more to these trips than just attending the ballet.

"Tom, I want you to find out all you can about these trips. I want to know if there's a real problem. In other words, just find out if the Prime Minster is getting too cozy with the Russians."

"All right, my wife Jenny and I will go to London tomorrow to see what we can find out about these trips. Is there anything else, sir?"

"No, Tom, just keep in touch with me and let me know what you find out. I'm not telling anyone else about what you are doing, so if anyone questions you, just tell them you are on a special assignment for the President.

"In case you didn't know, I promoted Ron Parsons to be the Director of the CIA. I'll tell Ron that you and Jenny are on an assignment for me so you will both be on the CIA payroll and expenses while you are working for me."

"Thank you , sir. I'm glad Ron finally got to be the Director of the CIA, he's a great guy and he will do a good job for the country. I'll keep in touch with you on your private phone number and email account. One more thing, would you please have your office send me a copy of your dossier on Prime Minster Blake Pearson?"

"Yes, I will have it sent to you today. Tom, I want to wish you good luck on this assignment. I guess this is a lot different assignment from what you normally get, but I know I can count on you and Jenny to get to the bottom of this mess. That is, if it's an actual mess which I hope it's not."

Jenny had been listening to Tom's side of the conversation and asked, "What is it that the President is calling you about this early on a Sunday morning?"

"Well, Jenny, the President is asking us to see if Blake Pearson, the Prime Minster of the United Kingdom, is playing footsie with the Russians or is he just taking the opportunity to be able to take his wife, Suri to see the ballets in Paris and Moscow on some rich Russian business man's money."

"The President woke us up this early on a Sunday morning to have us find out about the British Prime Minster's trips to see the ballet being paid for by some Russian business man?"

"Yeah, the President is concerned the Prime Minster maybe forgetting which side he's on and it's not supposed to be on the Russian's side."

Jenny replied, "The President is thinking a couple of trips paid for by a Russian business man for the Prime Minster and his wife to see a couple of ballets is going to change his thoughts about the UK supporting Russia instead of the USA?"

Tom replied, "Well, the President is concerned there maybe more to what's going on between the Prime Minster and the Russians, than just having the Prime Minister going to see ballets.

"OK, Tom when are we going to London?"

"I'll call Roger Dean and ask him to have the plane and his crew ready to fly us to London tomorrow."

Jenny asked, "Tom, what do you think about asking your folks to come out next week and stay with Tom Jr. and Jackie while we're gone?"

"I think they would love to come. That is, if I can get Dad to give up a few of his golf games with his buddies. I know Robert and Lily can take care of Tommy, but it would be good for my folks to come out to be with Tommy and Jackie. I want my folks to know our kids better."

Jenny replied, "Tom, you know Robert and Lily can take care of Tommy and Jackie is gone all the time working with her Hollywood clients. It seems like she's with them every day and now she's with them a lot of nights. You know, we hardly see her when we're home. She's so busy all of the times with all of those actors she works for."

"Jenny, you know I never had any idea that actors had to have their lawyers do so much work for them. Seems like they can hardly do anything for themselves, their contracts, and only God knows what other problems they get into that they need a lawyer for.

"Then there are people who are always trying to sue them for speaking to them or something just as crazy as that. You know that happens, only because actors are very well paid. So everybody is trying to get money from them any way they can."

"Tom, you know, she really loves all of this. Sometimes, I don't know if she loves looking after them or just likes to be with all of these pretty people."

"Jenny, maybe it's the other way around. Jackie is a beautiful, young, smart woman and God knows these people know you are one of the richest people in the world. If they could get her to marry one of them, they would never have to worry about having to keep getting jobs or keep working to keep up their life style."

"Tom, you have a suspicious mind. Is that why you married me, because I have money?"

"You know better than that. You knew I had enough money to do about anything I ever wanted to do in life. I just had to have you because I loved you so much and you make my life complete."

As Tom finished saying that, he reached down to Jenny. Then he pulled her straight up out of bed and into his arms and began kissing her.

They were soon back on the bed and found they had more important things to do than to keep worry about money or Russians or anything else in this world.

CHAPTER TWO

MAKING ARRANGEMENTS FOR FLYING TO LONDON

Later that day, Tom called Roger Dean, their pilot, and asked him to contact the rest of his crew and get their Gulfstream 550 plane ready to fly to London tomorrow afternoon.

Roger told him he would have his crew and the plane ready to go tomorrow by one pm.

Tom asked Roger if he still had the same crew that had been working for him for several years now.

Roger laughed and replied, "Yeah, I still have Tim Turpin as my Co-Pilot and Julia Meyers and Crystal Swan as your stewardesses. Are you crazy? Tom, this is the best job any one of us has ever had. Sometimes we go weeks and you never have us fly you anywhere and we get paid just the same as we did if we were working.

"Besides, we all love you, Jenny, Tom Jr. and Jackie. Plus, when we go with you, we get to go places where most of us have never been or had ever thought about going."

Tom replied, "Well, with all of the things we've put you through. We feel we owe you everything you get paid. Not too many pilots and their crew have to land in the Arctic Ocean just because some terrorist wanted to kill me."

"Well, it's not every crew that gets saved because their boss works for the CIA and has a chip embedded in their shoulder. So, we all feel like we are part of your family. Every one of us appreciates what you and Jenny do for us and for our country."

"Well, Roger, we feel the same way about you and your crew. We hope you can all keep working with us as long as you want to or need to."

Roger replied, "OK, boss, we'll see you tomorrow at the airport with everything and everybody ready to leave by one o'clock."

"Thanks, Roger, see you tomorrow."

Tom wasn't worried about their plane being sabotaged again, as it was when it was parked at the Cathy Pacific hanger at Los Angeles International Airport. It had been over a year since their plane went down in the Arctic Ocean, crashing only because people who used to work at the facility where they kept their plane had been paid to let someone sabotage their plane.

The CIA now had it kept in a fenced off area of the hanger and monitored by cameras connected to CIA Headquarters both in LA and the DC Area.

Plus, the gate was kept locked. Only Roger Dean and Tom had keys to unlock the CIA special locks. No more having their plane going down in the Arctic Ocean.

Once was enough for Tom, and it was certainly a miracle that Tom and his family and the crew survived the first time.

They wouldn't have except for one thing and that was that Tom had a CIA ID chip implanted in his left shoulder. They certainly would have all died in that cold water if it had not been for the CIA and the quick action of the US Coast Guard getting to their location and plucking them out of the icy cold water of the Arctic Ocean.

The CIA wanted to be sure they could find their luckiest agent anywhere in the world so several years before that happened, they had a ID chip implanted in his shoulder. That way, by using their satellites, they could track his location anywhere and any time he was on this earth.

That wasn't the first time the CIA needed to be able to locate Tom. He was sometimes pretty hard to keep up with him on so many of his assignments.

Tom knew at this time that he was one of only a few CIA Agents that had such a device implanted into their shoulder.

Later in the day, Tom got an email from the President's office with a complete dossier on Prime Minister Blake Pearson. Tom downloaded a copy of the document and then printed it off. It was twenty pages of information regarding Blake Pearson.

The dossier began with detailed information on his great grandparents, then his grandparents, next it covered his parents, and included his older brother and sister. Everything about his birth, schooling, friends, classmates, girl friends, the clubs he belonged to, his family's business, the family's wealth, any lawsuits, military service, his height and weight, and things that he liked and disliked.

Tom thought to himself, how did they miss the number of sheets of toilet paper he used on an average day? They certainly hadn't missed anything else.

First bit of information was that Blake was born at his family's country estate in York, he was the youngest son and he had an older brother and sister, Reginald and Elizabeth. Blake was twelve years younger that his brother and ten years younger than his sister.

His father and mother were both children of parents that were major shareholders in several banks in the UK. In many cases, some of their great-great grandfathers were original founders of these banks. So, banking was where all of the men in the family, on both sides of Blake Pearson's parents, were involved in banking either as a president of the banks or chairman of the board or directors of these banks.

So, to Tom it was obvious that money wasn't really a factor in the Prime Minister's making or not making trips to take his wife to the ballet.

The dossier said Blake was six-feet two inches tall and weighed one hundred seventy- five pounds. He had light brown hair, blue eyes and had a small scar on his lower left cheek, caused by getting hit with a cricket bat when he was fourteen.

He played cricket and golf in high school and college. He was so good at cricket he was offered a job with a couple of professional teams and in golf he was rated as one of the best players in England. He had won several championship playing in college golf, including having five holes-in-one in team play.

Blake's education was at the best schools that England had to offer: Eaton, then to Oxford, where he majored in business administration. He graduated at the top of his class at both Eaton and Oxford so it seemed like he was the best at everything he did.

He was always very popular with the girls, but one that was always by his side was Suri Evans. Who after working for years to become a ballerina was injured in a skiing accident in Switzerland and that ended her chance of becoming a ballerina.

Very soon after her recovery from her skiing accident, Blake asked her to become his wife and he didn't have to ask her a second time before she said yes.

They were married on a June day at Westminster Cathedral. They honeymooned on a large private yacht for four months. Traveling from England to the USA and then cruising along the eastern coast of America, from Boston to Key West, then off to travel the Caribbean, and then back to England.

Suri's folks were also in an old established business, just as Blake's. Her father, C.W. Evans, was the president of Lloyd's of London, one of the oldest and most prestigious companies in the world at providing insurance for shipping companies and it was one of the best known companies in the world.

Suri's mother was also from a successful family business; they were in the shipping business and they had interest in several British shipping companies.

After Blake and Suri's honeymoon, Blake took a job working with his best friend, Hanson Churchill, the Mayor of London, as an aide involved with public relations with foreign diplomats.

The mayor soon saw that Blake had everything needed to go into politics. He was well-spoken, good-looking and drew attention wherever he went. The mayor convinced Blake to run for a councilman's position in the coming election. Blake won in a walk.

From that experience, the ruling party asked him to run for a position in the federal government. He out-poled every candidate running for election, so as the next step a few years later, he would run for the Prime Minister's job. Same results, he won with a two-to-one margin.

As Prime Minster, he performed very well leading the government, along with having the best public support since what Winston Churchill had during World War II.

Reading all of this, Tom wondered, why or how would anyone ever even think he was becoming too cozy with the Russian Government.

Nothing in this twenty-page report would indicate that Blake Pearson was anything but a solid British citizen, no money problems, and no girls on the side.

Tom couldn't see anything that jumped out to him about Blake Pearson as being a potential threat of helping the Russians against the USA in any way or any time.

Tom guessed that was why he and Jenny were on their way to London, to see if the Prime Minister and his wife's trips to the ballets indicated anything more than just them seeing a couple of ballet performances as guests of someone they seemed to enjoy being with.

One thing Blake's dossier didn't cover was much information on his close friends or colleagues, such as Hanson Churchill.

Tom quickly sent a message back to the President's office requesting a dossier on Hanson Churchill and any other close friends of Blake Pearson.

CHAPTER THREE

CALL TO DAD TO STAY WITH TOMMY

Tom telephoned his folks and asked them if they would come to Beverly Hills and stay with Tommy while they went on an assignment for the President.

His dad, being a retired Army three-star general, didn't even ask what Tom and Jenny would be doing for the President, since he already knew that Tom couldn't discuss what their assignment was working for the President.

Josh asked Tom when they would they be leaving on their assignment?

Tom replied that they would be leaving tomorrow afternoon.

His dad said, "I have a golf game this afternoon, but we could fly out tomorrow to be with Tommy and Jackie while you're gone. I know you have no idea how long you will be gone, but since I lost so many of my golf partners, your mother and I can stay as long as you want us."

"You know, Son, it's not really good getting to be an old man. It seems like every month or so one of my old Army buddies dies off on me. So I've lost another golf partner to play golf with. Now I'm running out of guys to play golf with."

Tom replied, "Dad, you know we have a lot of room in our Beverly Hills estate and I really wish you and mom would just consider living here with us all the time. Then you wouldn't have to take care of your home and mom wouldn't have to do all of the cooking and taking care of the house."

"Tom, you know, Son, we might just take you up on that offer since we have lost so many of our friends. You are our only child and we don't get to see you much. I know it's hard to believe, but we miss seeing you and your family. We really never thought you would ever have a family after you lost your first love when she married somebody else when you were fighting in Vietnam."

"Well, dad, I certainly have a wonderful wife now and a son and a step-daughter, and we would love to have you and mom here with us all the time."

"OK, Tom. I'll talk it over with your mom so I can to see what she thinks about us moving to California and living with you. We have talked about it before, but I was the one who didn't want to move away from all of my buddies."

"Good! Dad. I know Jenny would love to have you and mom here with us. I know she only wishes her folks would come here, too, but we had to move them and her other in-laws from Hong Kong to Singapore since the Chinese communists have taken over. They just couldn't run her business from there anymore."

"Tell Jenny I'm sorry her folks had to leave Hong Kong. I know they loved it there since they were involved in so many businesses there."

"Yeah, Dad, they lost millions of dollars by selling all of the property they owned in Hong Kong. Jenny was the biggest loser since she owned far more property there. I don't know for sure, but I'm guessing she lost at least a billion dollars when she sold all of her property there."

"Wow, that's a lot of money, son. I hope she's not having any mental problems over losing so much money."

"No, Dad, she's doing OK, far better than just doing OK. She is still one of the richest people in the world. I don't get involved in her business, but I know she still has several more billions of dollars of real estate around the world. She still earns more money than most of the countries in the world do every month."

"They have a problem unlike most of the world's population. They have to keep buying more businesses so they don't have too much money that just keeps piling up in their banks. They want to keep the money working to provide jobs with decent salaries and benefits for their employees and their families."

"So, Dad, she's not worried about losing a billion dollars on the property that she sold short, as she calls it, but she was very sad about selling the building her first husband built for her, with her apartment overlooking Hong Kong Bay. She loved that view and so did I."

Josh replied, "Son, you know she could still build a building just like the one she had if she wanted to. She could just have another one built like her old building somewhere around Los Angeles."

"I don't think she would ever do that, but I guess I don't really know what she would do. She does whatever she wants to in her business and I would be the last one to try to suggest something about operating her business. She probably knew more about running a business when she was twelve years old than I do today. Besides all of that, she's a lawyer, and all I know is life in the Army and working for the CIA, and now she is a CIA Agent to boot."

"Well, Son, I've heard you're the tops at what you do and you're the person the President of the United States calls when he's got a problem. So I think your pretty special, too."

"Thanks, Dad, but maybe you're a little prejudiced since I followed in your footsteps."

"Well it was a great choice for America and I'm glad you did but I was never a CIA Agent."

"I guessed you missed out on that one. I love you, Dad, but I've got to get going to make all of the plans to leave for London tomorrow. Love you and mom and we will be very happy if you both decide to live here in California with us. See you soon."

"One last question before you go, do you have any idea how long you're going to be gone?"

"Sorry, Dad, I don't have a clue. I don't know where this assignment is going to take us."

"OK, Son. I know I've been on some assignments like that in the past for the Army. Doesn't matter to your mom and me just as long as you and Jenny stay safe and we'll see you when you get home."

"Bye, Dad."

After Tom hung up the phone, he went into his walk-in safe and took out two Glock 19 guns and holsters along with several boxes of ammunition for Jenny and himself. After he had their weapons, Tom carefully closed the door and locked back up the walk-in safe.

The rest of the day was spent packing clothes for being gone for several days or weeks and for many different occasions. Everything for both Tom and Jenny from casual, formal and everything in between.

Of course they had plenty of help with Jenny's butler, Robert Fong, and his wife, Lily, who was Jenny's maid and had taken care of her since she was born. They still looked after Jenny as well as taking care of her daughter, Jackie Lu, and their son, Tommy.

For Jenny, they packed a large wardrobe trunk and one large suitcase and one smaller suitcase for her makeup and jewelry.

For Tom, they packed a large wardrobe trunk and a small duffle bag for his toiletries.

So before Sunday was over, everything was ready to go and was just waiting for them to leave on Monday morning.

Tom and Jenny spent most of their day with Tommy and playing games he liked to play.

Jackie was also home for most of the day, so she joined them playing with Tommy almost all afternoon. Then, Jackie had to get ready to go to some charity event with one of the movie stars she represented.

Before she left, she made a special effort to give Jenny a hug and kiss to wish her safe travel and a safe trip going and coming back home.

CHAPTER FOUR

FLYING TO LONDON AND STARTING THEIR ASSIGNMENT

Morning comes too quickly when you have to get up and get ready to go on an assignment and you have no idea of where it's going to take you or how long you're going to be gone. But, there they were, Tom and Jenny getting up and getting ready to fly to London, working for the President of the United States to see if the UK'S Prime Minster was getting involved with some sinister plot against America along with the Russians.

Tom said out loud, "We are getting ready to go to London for the President to see if the Prime Minster of the UK is somehow going to help Russia against America. Just saying that sounds so absurd, it's ridiculous. Yet, here we are, flying out to London to see if it true. Unbelievable!"

Jenny replied, "Well, Tom, maybe the Prime Minster is one of those Englishmen who is still unhappy about America breaking away from the British Empire."

"After all of this time, I really doubt that's his problem in today's world."

Jenny replied, "Well, nothing about this makes any sense. The Prime Minster and his wife seem to be happy, with no problems with money or prestige or lovers on the side for either one. Maybe it's just that the Prime Minster's wife loves the ballet so much and he just wants to take her to see the best ballet dancers in the world and that's all there is to it."

"I think you're right and just maybe they like this Russian business man and enjoy his company. I've met a few Russians that I've worked with that were all right."

They got themselves ready and had breakfast and watched as Robert had their luggage brought to the landing pad they had built for the helicopters to land in their back yard.

Tom and Jenny both searched through their minds to be sure they had packed everything they would need on their trip. Yeah, they did.

They gave kisses to Tommy and Jackie, and after everything was loaded in the helicopter, they boarded and were soon in the air, leaving Beverly Hills en route to LAX to board their jet.

True to his word, when the chopper landed near the hanger where their jet was kept they saw Captain Dean and his crew ready to join them and to get on their way to London.

Captain Dean told them they would be flying over the North Pole to London.

Tom said, "Sounds like a shorter flight and I can drop Santa a note telling him what I want for Christmas."

All the crew laughed and Captain Dean said, "Welcome aboard, we hope you get what you want for Christmas, Tom."

Tom replied, "Me too, maybe getting back home soon would be one thing I would like, with this assignment finished!"

Jenny replied, "Amen!"

So they were off.

Several hours later Tom heard Captain Dean say over the speaker, "We will be landing at London Stansted Airport in about one hour."

Sure enough, Tom could feel and hear the wheels going down on their jet and soon he could see them gliding just above the runway, then felt a slight bump when the wheels touched down on the runway.

They would be staying in central London at the Claridge Hotel and their crew would all be staying at the Hampton Hotel, Stansted Airport.

The crew could enjoy all of the sights of London and still be able to be ready for Tom or Jenny to go with just one phone call to let them know where and when they wanted to go.

Tom had made arrangements for a limo to pick Jenny and him up at the office of where their plane would be parked during their stay in London.

Tom asked Captain Dean before they left if they were all right, with enough money to buy their food and transportation while they were in London.

Captain Dean told him they wouldn't have any problems for money since all of them had American Express cards from Jenny's corporation, so they could get anything they needed. We just have to keep receipts and file our weekly reports after we get back home.

Tom turned around and a uniformed driver asked, "Are you General Parker?"

Tom replied, "Yes, sir I am."

The driver said, "Sir, your car is here."

Tom said, "Good, my wife and I are ready to go to our hotel."

"All right, sir, do you have luggage?"

"Yes, we do. They are just taking it out of our plane right now."

Just then two men brought their luggage in on a very large cart: one duffle bag, one small suitcase, two large suitcases and one large trunk.

The driver said, "Sir, I don't think we can get that large trunk into the limo."

"It's OK, take the suitcases and everything else in your car and I'll make arrangements to have the trunk delivered to our hotel."

The driver asked the men who brought in their luggage on a cart if they could get the luggage in the back of the limo.

After they helped load all of the luggage into the boot, as the English called the car's trunk, he thanked them for their help.

Then the driver came back into the office and asked, "Are you ready to go, General?"

Tom replied, "Just a few minutes more, my wife is on her phone talking to her office in Singapore."

Tom asked the operator of the hanger service if he could make arrangements to have the large trunk moved to the Claridge Hotel for them.

The manager said, "Yes, sir, I'll have it taken care of for you."

Jenny completed her call to Singapore and the two of them walked out to the very shiny black Rolls. The driver opened the door for Jenny and let her be seated before he closed the door. Tom told the driver that it was OK, he could take care of getting in the car by himself.

So the driver got behind the wheel of the Rolls and away they went, headed to the hotel.

As they rode along Tom said, "You know, Jenny, I miss riding in your Rolls, since you left it in Hong Kong. Yours was the first ride I ever had in a Rolls. I was very impressed. I think you ought to buy a new one when we get home. I'm sure Robert Fong misses it, too."

"So, you don't think our limo is a nice as the Rolls? OK, before we leave London going home I'll buy one and have it shipped to Beverly Hills."

"Good, I'll like that."

Traffic in London hadn't improved since the last time Tom was here and by the time they got to the Claridge Hotel, Tom looked up and saw a small truck parked in front of the hotel and Jenny's large trunk was in the process of being unloaded.

By the time the rest of the luggage was unloaded and they checked into the hotel their things were already in their suite with a staff member unpacking Jenny's clothes and hanging them up in her closets.

Tom told their driver they wouldn't need him any more tonight but they wanted him at the hotel tomorrow by ten o'clock in the morning with the limo.

The driver said, "I'm sorry, Sir, but I understood you only wanted a ride from the airport to the hotel."

Tom replied, "No, I have no idea how long we will be in London, but I would like you to be available every day and sometimes at night as long as we are here. Do you want to help us like this or should I ask for another driver?"

"No, sir, General, I would be honored to serve you, sir."

"Great, what's your name, driver?"

"It's Benny, General."

"OK, Benny, you've got a deal and you can just call me Tom and my wife's name is Jenny. We have a job to do while we are in London. It's important what we have to do and maybe there will be a lot of strange things we may do that you won't understand what we're doing, but it's a very important job and we will appreciate your help. Are we clear on everything, Benny?"

"Yes, sir, Mr. Tom. I'll be here in the morning before ten am and I will be ready to take you anywhere you want to go. Good night, sir.

"Good night, Benny, we'll see you in the morning."

By the time Tom returned to their suite, Jenny and her helper had everything unpacked and hung up in the closet and toiletry items in the bathrooms. One bathroom for Tom and one for Jenny.

They had dinner in their suite and soon after that, they were in bed so they could be ready for whatever came next.

Benny drove his limo to the parking lot to get ready to go home when one of the other drivers was just checking in. He asked, "So, what about the people you picked up today, what do they do?"

Benny replied, "I don't know, but it must be very important because he seems like he is doing some kind of investigation here in London."

"You mean he came to London in a private jet with just him as the passenger to do some kind of investigation?"

"No, his wife is with him, it seems like whatever he is investigating she's helping him and they are staying at the Claridge Hotel."

"It must be a really important investigation if somebody in London brought in a person like him, so it must be a really special job."

"Who knows? Maybe the Prime Minster hired him. You know he's got the kind of money that he could afford to hire a man like that."

Jimmy, the other driver Benny had been talking to, said he had to go to pick up a man at a restaurant.

When Jimmy picked up his client he remembered he had picked up this man several times and he knew he was very special. So Jimmy was telling him about some hot shot investigator that the Prime Minster hired to do some kind of investigation here in London and the guy was staying in the Claridge Hotel, that's got to be one of the most expensive hotels in London.

"Jimmy, do you know what the man's name is?"

"No, Your Highness, but I can check the log the company keeps and I've got a copy of today's log."

They soon arrived at the gentleman's residence and Jimmy said, "Your Highness, if you really want to know this man's name, I'll look it up for you if you like."

"Yeah, I would like to know what this VIP investigator's name is, if you think that would be all right?"

Jimmy replied, "It will be no problem for me to give it to you Your Highness. I'll look it up for you right now. Here it is, the guy's name is Tom Parker."

"Thank you, Jimmy, here's an extra hundred pounds for you. I always appreciate your help."

The following morning the man called a meeting with his top aides and told them what he found out about the Prime Minster hiring some hot shot investigator by the name of Tom Parker to investigate our activities. I told Al-Sadr to get rid of him.

CHAPTER FIVE

MEETING WITH AMBASSADOR STEVE JONES

After breakfast, Tom called Steve Jones and after a few minutes his secretary told Tom that Ambassador Jones would be with him in just a few minutes and to, please, hold the line.

Only a minute or so passed and Tom heard, "Good morning, this is Ambassador Jones.

Tom replied, "Good morning, Mr. Ambassador, this is CIA Agent Tom Parker here in London, as you have requested, to have someone check on certain activities of Prime Minster Blake Pearson. I'm wondering if you would have time to meet with my wife, CIA Agent Jenny Parker, and myself sometime today?"

"Yes sir, Agent Parker, I will make time to meet with you and Mrs. Parker. How about meeting you about one this afternoon for lunch at your hotel. I understand you are staying at the Claridge Hotel."

"Yes, that's where we are staying and that would be excellent. I'll make reservations for the three of us."

"Great, I'll see you at one at the restaurant."

After Tom finished his call, he told Jenny, "We'll be meeting the Ambassador for lunch at one this afternoon here at our hotel."

A few minutes before one o'clock, Tom and Jenny were seated at a small round table designed for four people. Tom told the waiter there would only be three of them for lunch

So, the waiter picked up the extra plate and glasses from the table before Ambassador Pearson arrived and removed the fourth chair.

As soon as he arrived at the restaurant, he was taken to their table.

Tom stood up and introduced himself and Jenny to the Ambassador.

Steve Jones reached out his right hand toward Tom and the two of them shook hands and Tom asked the Ambassador to please have a seat, and he promptly sat down between Tom and Jenny.

The Ambassador said, "I appreciate you both coming to England to look into this problem with the Prime Minister's relationship with the Russians."

Tom said, "Jenny and I are always ready to help with any problem the good ole USA may have at any time or any place if we can."

"Well, that's kind of the problem. I don't know if we have a real problem with the Prime Minister's relationship with the Russians or not ,but we don't want to ever have a major problem between us and the UK government, so you will have to be very careful handling this potential problem."

Tom replied, "I understand that, but what makes you think these trips that the Prime Minster and his wife are taking with this Russian business man, Peter Valkovich, are anything but more than a chance for the Prime Minster's wife, Suri to attend these performances.

"I guess it's the timing, plus with the war going on in the Ukraine, it's causing me to question the Prime Minster and his wife going off with a Russian businessman to attend these ballets."

"OK, that's what Jenny and I are here to find out about. Do you know if anybody else from the Prime Minster's office goes along on these trips?"

"I don't really know, but I would guess if anyone did, it would be Hanson Churchill, the Prime Minster's best friend. He generally doesn't ever let Blake out of his sight."

Jenny asked, "Have these two been friends for a long time?"

"I believe they have since they were young children, Hanson parents were killed and Blake's folks took Hanson in to raise along with Blake."

Tom asked, "That's a big responsibility to take on, someone else's child to raise."

"Well, I guess Hanson's folks actually worked for the Pearson's and were killed when some drunk diver ran his truck over them while working for the Pearson's. So they took over the responsibility of raising the boy."

Jenny asked, "Did Hanson go to the same schools as Blake did?"

"They started out together, but Hanson wasn't the scholar Blake was, so he couldn't get into the same schools that Blake did, but they kept up their relationship all of those years."

By the time they finished their lunch, the Ambassador said he had to get back to his office for a staff meeting.

Tom told the Ambassador before he left, that he and Jenny would try to set up a meeting with Prime Minister Pearson for Jenny to talk about setting up some of her businesses in the UK. She would want to see if their were any perks for her to establish some of her businesses here.

"She will be talking about moving some of her businesses to Europe, which would be a big deal for almost any country in Europe. Getting one of her companies established in England would certainly be a big boost in their economy. They would be exporting a lot of different products out of the country, which would give England a huge source of income for the workers hired here and the shipping companies she would be doing business with. Plus, the country would get a lot of new tax money."

Jenny had called the Prime Minister's office and asked if she could set up a meeting with the Prime Minister and was politely told that the Prime Minister was very busy; perhaps it would be better if she called for an appointment with the trade minister.

Jenny was just as polite and asked, "Would you please ask the Prime Minister if he would consider calling Jenny Parker" and gave the lady her cell number.

Twenty minutes later, Jenny's cell phone signaled an incoming call.

When she answered the call, a woman said, "Mrs. Parker, would you please hold while I connect you with Prime Minster Blake Pearson."

"Yes, thank you."

The next thing she heard was Prime Minster Pearson speaking, "Good Morning, Mrs. Parker, how may I help you? I understand from my secretary that you might be considering setting up some of your businesses in the U.K."

"Yes, Prime Minster, I am considering moving some of my companies to Europe after closing all of my holdings in Hong Kong due to the Chinese from Beijing taking over the Hong Kong government."

"I would certainly be willing to make time to meet with you. Just tell me when you would like to meet me, Mrs. Parker."

"Please, Prime Minster, it's just Jenny."

"OK, Jenny, I'm Blake."

"Good, my husband Tom and I will be here in London for several days so you just tell me when you have time and I'll make it work, OK, Blake?"

"How about tomorrow, maybe we could have lunch together along with our spouses?"

"That would be great, Blake. I look forward to meeting you and your wife."

"Well I'll certainly be happy to have the opportunity to meet you and your husband. I would like you to come for lunch at 10 Downing Street at one o'clock tomorrow."

"Thank you and I'll certainly be able to remember your address, it has to be one of the best known addresses in the world."

Blake chuckled and replied, "Yes, I guess it is. Since it's been the home and office for the British Prime Minster for so many years, it's a little like saying the White House. Everybody in the world certainly knows who lives and works there."

Jenny responded, "Yes, that's certainly true and we do look forward to see you and number 10 Downing Street."

After she hit the off switch on her cell phone, she said, "OK, Tom, we have a meeting with Prime Minster Blake Pearson and his wife for lunch at number 10 Downing Street tomorrow at one."

"Good job, Jenny, no other CIA agent would be able to get that kind of invitation for lunch with the Prime Minister of England and at his home. Great job, Jenny."

Later that day, Jenny decided she needed to buy a new car if they were going to be operating a business in London. She called up the Rolls dealer in London and asked if they had any new Rolls Royce cars available. The answer was, yes, they had a few cars in stock and she asked about their colors. They told her they had black and a silver colored one. She said, "I think I would like the silver-colored one since I have a black one in America."

Less than two hours later, she purchased the silver Rolls Royce and hired the driver, Benny, who had driven them when he worked for the limo Service. Benny knew London very well since he originally trained to be a taxi driver.

In order to get a license to drive a taxi in London you had to be able to know the city well enough for you to be able to pass a test proving that no matter where you wanted to go you could get there. The new potential taxi driver had to be able to tell you the best route to travel to get to any destination in the London area.

Many people had to study for years learning the city well enough to pass this test.

They often rode bicycles to learn the streets and how to go from one point to another.

Tom wondered that since they now had GPS systems, if they still had to be able to pass this same test. He thought probably not anymore.

However, Tom asked their driver, Benny, if he had to pass the old test. He told them he began driving taxies several years before GPS devices arrived, so, yes, he did.

The following day, Tom and Jenny arrived at number 10 Downing Street at 12:45 PM in their new silver Rolls Royce and made their way to the front door.

Tom pushed the doorbell button and the door was soon answered by Blake Pearson.

Blake said, "Hello, Jenny, I bet this is your husband Tom," as he extended his hand toward Tom. Tom met his hand with his own hand and grasped it firmly and shook hands with Blake.

Tom released his hand and Blake said, "Please come into my borrowed home, you know, the one owned by the people of the UK."

Tom laughed thinking to himself, no American President would ever say that about the White House. Once they were elected, they thought they owned the place. Big difference between England and America. The English Prime Minster knew he was just a guest in their country's house. Tom liked that.

Soon Blake Pearson introduced his wife Suri to Jenny and Tom.

Tom thought she carried herself as a royal personage the way she glided over to greet Jenny and Tom. Tom had had occasions to see British royalty during his military career when being presented medals for his service in the middle East.

Jenny thought Suri must surely have some royal blood in her for the same reason that Tom thought so. But they soon found out what she had was the pure blue blood of the highest upper class of English wealth.

Maybe they didn't have the money and income that Jenny and her folks had today, but Suri's family had it many centuries before Jenny's family.

Their lunch was wonderful and both Tom and Jenny were super impressed with both Blake and Suri. By the time lunch ended they were very sure that Blake and Suri were, as the old cowboy movie use to say, not in cohoots with anyone. Jenny asked Suri, "We were told you were a rising star in ballet, what happened to you to decide to give that up?"

Suri replied, "Oh, I didn't have any say in that, I'm sorry to say. I managed to get myself hurt and that ended my dream of becoming a premier ballerina. So I married Blake and became a housewife."

With that statement, Blake said, "Yeah, she married me and became a housewife and a Good Will Ambassador for Mother England and I don't have any idea how many other things she has to do as the wife of the Prime Minster. It seems like she is more in demand than I am."

"Blake, you know I just do what your people tell me to do and when and where to do it."

Tom said, "Well, it sounds like you two have your jobs cut out for you."

Blake replied, "Boy, that's true. It seems like both of us are going in different directions every day."

Jenny asked, "Do you ever just get to do something you both like to do?"

Suri answered, "Well, we did get to go to a ballet or two together."

Blake said, "Yeah, only because we have a friend who is a Russian business man who loves the ballet and he has invited us to go with him a couple of times."

Tom asked, "How did you get to know a Russian business man?"

Blake replied, "Well, I met him while I was running for the Prime Minster's job and he gave me some insight on dealing with the problems dealing with the Russia Government, but I have to say it only get worse every day."

Tom said, "I sorry to hear that, why do you think that is?"

"Well, the Soviet Union had a huge amount of territory and it has slowly lost so much of its area and people. The leaders of Russia think the West is the cause of all of that, but who really knows all the reasons. I only know they think we, the West, are trying to cut it down so it's not a power in the world anymore."

Then Blake said, "Jenny, we didn't get to have much of a conversation about your thoughts of establishing some of your company's operations here in England."

Jenny replied, "No, we didn't, but I feel like after spending time with you and your wife and getting to look around, I believe London would be an ideal location for my companies. Tom and I will be checking out locations for my potential headquarters and warehouse for our operations for Europe."

Blake said, "Please let me know if there is anything I could do to help you."

Jenny answered, "Well, some governments have offered us some incentives to establish our business in their country, like lower taxes or low-cost government bonds which would always be appreciated to help us with construction of new facilities.

"Jenny, do you have any idea how many employees your new facilities may need for your business?"

"Blake, I can't say for sure, but I would guess somewhere around a thousand employees. We will also have to bring in some of our folks to supervise the operations. I'm sure I will need your help to get these folks into your country with permanent visas. This may amount to as many as forty employees and their families."

"I'm sure with proper documentation that shouldn't be a problem."

"Most of these people will be coming from Hong Kong and some may have British passports already. After I have time to check available facilities, I would like to get back with you and give you full details on my plans.

Blake replied, "If my office can be of any help, just give me a ring."

Tom said, "Before we leave, I would like to invite both of you for dinner at Claridge later this week if you can find time; just call me or Jenny and let us know which day you can make it."

"OK, Tom, either Suri or I will give you a call later this week."

Tom said, "You know, Blake, sometime I would like to meet your Russian friend. I worked with several Russian KGB men in the past when we were searching for terrorists. I would like to know if your friend is anything like those guys. Man, they were afraid of their own shadow that someone would turn them in for spending one more ruble then necessary."

"Well, Tom, I don't think Peter is anything like your KGB fellows. In the first place he grew up in Paris and the South of France where his father served as a Russian diplomat. Maybe I could get Peter to have lunch with you at your hotel someday this week."

"Thanks, Blake. I would like that a lot. It should be very interesting."

CHAPTER SIX

SETTING UP A MEETING WITH PETER VALKOVICH

Two days later, Tom got a telephone call from Peter Valkovich who said, "Hello, Tom Parker. I understand from Blake Pearson you would like to meet me."

Tom replied, "Yes, I would be delighted to meet you if you have time while my wife Jenny and I are in London."

"I understand you used to be with the CIA and you worked at some point with some KGB agents. Blake said you wanted to see if I was as nervous as those fellows were."

Tom laughed and said, "Well, I doubt that you are, but the other thing I really want to talk with you about is to see if there might be an opportunity for you to do some work with Jenny's company's by either selling some of your products through her company or you selling some of hers. I know the Pearson's are very impressed with you."

"That's very nice to hear. I think they are very special people."

"OK, Peter, do you have a day this week that you could have lunch with Jenny and me?"

"Well, I could have lunch with you tomorrow. Could I just meet you for lunch at your hotel, because I love eating at the Claridge. Back before I bought an apartment in London I used to live at the Claridge."

"Great, Peter, is one o'clock for lunch OK for you?"

"That will be fine, so I'll see you at one tomorrow."

Tom hung up the phone and said, "OK, Jenny, we're have a lunch meeting with Peter Valkovich tomorrow here at the hotel."

Jenny replied, "Well, that should be very interesting, I'm anxious to see how Mr. Peter Valkovich looks and talks. I heard what you told him about him maybe working with my company. So, I guess I'm going to be the one to do most of talking during of our meeting with him, is that right?"

"Correct, my dear, you're the boss of your company, I'm just a tag-a-long."

"Well, you are a very nice tag-a-long and I love you a lot."

"Always good to hear. Since I feel the same way about you, maybe we should get married."

Jenny turned her wedding ring around on her finger and said, "We are already did that don't you remember?"

"Good, I'm really glad we did that. You know, being my age you forget so many things. As he held her in his arms and softly kissed her, he said, "I love you so much."

Then the room phone rang and Tom picked it up and said, "Tom Parker here."

The voice on the other end of the call said in not very good English, "I know why you're here and it's going to be the death of you and your wife."

Then Tom heard the telephone being hung up.

Tom turned to Jenny and she asked, "Who was that, Tom?"

"I have no idea, but the voice said "I know why you are here and it's going to be the death of you and your wife."

Jenny said, "Wow, have you ever had a call anything like that one?"

"No, I haven't. I've had plenty of people tell me they were going to kill me, but never over the phone. They were generally holding a gun and shooting at me, but so far I'm still alive."

Tom picked up his cell phone and called the CIA's London office.

Tom asked for the agent in charge of the office and told the person who answered the phone that his name was Tom Parker with the CIA and he was in London on a special assignment and wanted to speak with the London Director of the CIA.

A few minutes passed and then he heard a man say,"Hello, Tom Parker, this is Robert Clark. I'm the CIA Chief of the London office, how can I help you?"

Tom replied, "Chief Clark, this is CIA Agent Tom Parker along with my wife, Agent Jenny Parker, and we are here on a special assignment for the President and I need your help."

"How can I help you?"

"I just got a call on my room phone threatening to kill Jenny and myself and I thought maybe you could help look into this call to see if we can find out who made that call and where the call was made from."

"Where are you, Agent Parker?"

"We're staying at the Claridge Hotel in downtown London."

"Well, that's a pretty good place to be staying for CIA Agents."

"Yes, it is, but my wife is used to staying in this kind of hotel, since she's more of a business owner than a CIA Agent."

"OK, Agent Parker, we will be over to your hotel in about thirty minutes and see what we can find out about your call."

Just about thirty minutes later they heard someone knocking on their door.

Tom put his gun in his left hand, hiding it behind the door when he opened it and saw two men standing at their door.

The man closest to the open door said, "Tom Parker, I'm Robert Clark and this is Agent Roy Rogers and, no, he's not a singing cowboy, just a good CIA Agent."

Tom had to laugh a little even if Jenny and he had just been told they were going to die and said, "Come in, gentlemen, but, Roy will have to leave Trigger in the lobby."

That made both agents laugh as they were coming into Tom and Jenny's suite and Robert said, "Well, I'm glad you can still laugh a little even after being threatened this morning."

Tom extended his right hand and shook hands with Robert and Roy and said, "We appreciate you coming over to help us check this call out."

Robert said, "We're not very happy to have a couple of CIA Agents threatened in our territory, so we're here to see if we can help."

"Thank you, we do appreciate your help and I'm not very happy that someone knows where we are staying and has the nerve to call our room and tell me they are going to kill us."

Robert asked, "Can you tell us what kind of an assignment you are on for the President, but if you can't, we will understand that too."

"No, I'm sorry we can't, but I can tell you it involves a high ranking British official."

"Yes, we understand but I think I know that it is the Prime Minster, we've sent in several reports that he's very cozy with a Russian business man."

Tom replied, "Yes, that's what we are here for. Your reports have gone to the President so he sent us here to see what we can find out about this friendship and the Russian business man."

Robert said, "Well, I'm glad somebody is concerned enough to have someone check it out. I'm sure we could have done it, but I'm glad the President, is following up on this before we are blind-sided on this.

"We don't know what the Prime Minister might tell him, so we are worried about a lot of security for our armed forces and our allies."

Tom asked, "Do you think the Prime Minister would do this to help the Russians?'

"No, we don't think he would do it on purpose, but just a slip of the tongue might tell too much. We just don't know, but are concerned because the Prime Minster and his

wife go off with this guy on trips to Paris and even Moscow lasting several days."

"Well, my wife and I have just met the Prime Minster and his wife and he will be working with my wife, Jenny, to help her move one of her companies to England. We will see how he reacts around Mr. Valkovich, since Mr. Pearson suggested Jenny work with him to take a look at some of the warehouse areas of London."

Robert said, "I think we better move you and Jenny somewhere else so the guy who threatened you won't know where you live."

"I think you're right, do you have any idea where we might go?"

"Yes," Robert said, "The company has an apartment in the same building our office is in, if you can get your things packed up we'll get everything moved over to it."

Jenny said, "OK, that sounds good but it might take me longer than an hour to get all of my things ready to move."

"Not a problem. I'll have one of our staff workers come over and help you and then she can coordinate the movers to get you to your new apartment."

"Thanks, Robert. I'm sorry to be such a problem, but I have to have a lot of different clothes. Since I never know what we may be doing or have to dress up for some formal occasion."

Robert replied, "I've got to get back to the office right now, but I'll have Roy stay with you as a back-up in case this guy who threatened you tries anything before we can get you moved."

Tom said, "You don't need to do that. I'm sure we can take care of this ourselves."

"Sure, you can, but having an extra man around can't hurt anything."

"OK, then we will let Roy help take care of us."

Then Tom said to Jenny, "I've got to tell our driver Benny where we are going to be living so I think I better have him come here and help us get moved. Then he will know where we are going to be staying. I'm glad he has a place to park the Rolls at night so it not parked out on the street."

Tom called Benny and about thirty minutes later he was knocking on their suite's door.

Roy said, "I'll get the door as he pulled out his weapon, before he opened the door to let Benny in the suite.

Tom said, "It's OK, Roy, he's our driver."

Benny came in and saw Roy putting his weapon back in its holster and said, "Mr. Parker, is everything OK?"

Tom said, "Yes, Benny, it's OK, Roy is here to help keep us safe since someone threatened to kill us, so we are moving to an apartment."

A few minutes later, someone else knocked on their door and Roy did the same thing before he opened the door, he had his weapon ready.

When the door opened he saw the woman, Mary, who worked at the CIA office along with two moving company employees.

The woman said, "It's OK, Roy, these men are my brothers and they run a moving company and they are here to take all of the Parker's thing over to the company's apartment.

Less than an hour later everything was packed and loaded in the moving van. Then Tom checked out of their suite, while Roy continued standing a little way back from Tom and Jenny to be sure no one came up close to them.

After Tom finished checking out of their suite, the four of them walked directly to the limo where another CIA agent was keeping watch over their Rolls. Tom, Jenny, Roy and the lady from the CIA office, Mary, all got into the car.

Roy sat up front with Benny and gave him directions to go to the CIA's apartment.

It took almost forty minutes before they arrived at the building where the CIA's London office was located and where their new apartment was.

This building also had a parking garage, so they could drive through a security gate that only the CIA cars could open. However, they gave Benny a hand-held device that he could use to open the steel security gate.

In addition, the whole outside of the building was covered by security cameras to protect the building and the people who worked there.

After Benny had the limo through the parking gate, Roy told him to keep driving to the top floor of the parking garage which would be close to the CIA apartment. Benny had to use two parking spaces to get the Rolls out of the traffic lane.

Roy told him it would be all right because they only had a few cars that came up to this floor of the parking garage.

After they got out of the limo, Mary gave Tom and Jenny a key that let them into the inside of the building to be able to go to their new apartment.

Mary told Benny she would have to get him another key so he could also have a way to get into the hallway to go to Tom and Jenny's apartment.

Mary unlocked the door and led them past several doors until the came to a door that had a sign that said, "Private--No Entry."

Mary put a key in to the door lock and turned the key and the door opened and Mary walked through the door and switched on the lights.

Tom and Jenny saw a very nicely furnished living and dining room.

Mary showed them around the apartment, besides the large living and dining room the apartment had a kitchen, two bedrooms and two bathrooms, plus another bathroom in the hallway for guests.

Jenny was very impressed with the layout of the apartment and the details of the furniture and the kitchen with very nice dishes and silverware.

Jenny asked Mary how come this apartment was so nicely furnished and so well equipped?

Mary explained it was done this way in case the President ever had to have a safe secure place to stay during a visit to London.

She added, "It's never been used, so you are the first people to ever stay here."

Jenny thanked her for the information.

Tom would later find out this building was owned by the CIA and the outside of the building was designed to look just like the other three buildings on this corner that were low-cost office buildings.

Mary's brothers soon brought all of their things that had been taken from their hotel suite, and Mary helped Jenny unpack and hang up her and Tom's clothes in the two large closets.

After every one left, Jenny said, "Well, it's not the Claridge Hotel, but it's a pretty nice place that we are getting to stay in with a lot of security."

Tom replied, "It's certainly better than so many places that I've stayed and like you said, it certainly has to be one of the most secure places I have ever stayed in."

The following morning as they were having their coffee, their door bell rang and Tom went to the door and Robert Clark was at the door.

Tom said, "Come in, Robert, how are you this morning?"

"I'm doing OK."

Robert put down a copy of the London Times Newspaper on their kitchen table and the headlines on the front page read, "Couple Murdered At the Claridge Hotel."

Tom said, "Oh, my God, Jenny. A couple were murdered at the Claridge Hotel last night."

Tom read the short story to her about the murders. A couple were killed last night at the Claridge Hotel in their room. The police reported that the couple had just checked into the hotel last night after arriving from the United States. The names of the victims have not been identified pending notification of the next of kin."

Jenny said, "That's awful, it could have been us."

Tom replied, "Well, if they had tried to kill us, we might have been able to kill them. I feel so bad about having someone killed when I'm sure they were trying to kill us."

Robert said, "Well, we know one thing for sure, whoever was responsible for trying to kill you will not be happy that they killed the wrong people."

Tom replied, "They will be really upset when I kill them, because I'll find them, you can bet on that, and I'll kill them."

C H A P T E R   S E V E N

MEETING WITH PETER VALKOVICH

om told Jenny, "We are going to have to get moving if we make it back to the Claridge Hotel to meet Peter Valkovich for lunch at one. I want to be seated in the restaurant waiting for him, so he doesn't know that we have checked out of the hotel or that we had moved to a different suite."

Jenny replied, "Good idea, if he doesn't meet us, then we will have a good idea that he knew we were going to be killed."

"That's right, my love,"

They had Benny drive them to the hotel to meet Peter for their lunch and to be sure they were in the restaurant before one o'clock.

Benny got them there about fifteen minutes before one and they hurried into the hotel and into the restaurant. Tom asked the head waiter to please give them a table for three, where they could talk without having too many other people being able to overhear their conversation.

He took them to a table that was near the back of the restaurant that only had about three tables. Their table also gave them a good view of everyone who came into the restaurant and it wasn't near any other tables. He said to Tom, "I'll be sure not to seat anyone else in this area."

Tom thanked him and gave him a twenty pound note. The waiter thanked him and said, "I'll be sure to bring your guest over to you when he arrives,"

He then said, "You are Mr. and Mrs. Parker, aren't you?"

Tom said, "That's right, how did you know our name?"

The waiter replied, "I've seated you a couple of times before during your stay and you and your wife are certainly a very handsome couple."

Tom thanked him for his help and the nice thing he had said about them.

They had only been seated a short time before the waiter brought a tall, well-dressed man over to their table and said, "Your guest, Mr. Valkovich, has arrived.,"

Tom stood up and said, "Peter, how do you do?"

Then Tom extended his right hand and shook hands with Peter.

Peter replied, "Hello, Tom. How are you, Mrs. Parker?"

Jenny replied, "I'm just fine and I certainly appreciate you taking time to visit with me. Please sit down."

Peter sat down and said, "I can't believe the awful news about a couple of people being killed here in the Claridge last night. Did you hear anything when this went on? It's just unbelievable that something like that could happen in this hotel."

Tom said, "No, we didn't know anything about it until this morning. I'm telling you, it's not safe to be anywhere in this world anymore."

"Well, the Times didn't give many details about how the couple were killed or what their names were, just that they were from America."

Jenny said, "Can we please change the subject? I would like to have a nice lunch without anything else being said about people being killed in the hotel."

Peter replied, "Yes, I would certainly be glad to talk about what I might be able to do to help you with your business here in the UK or Europe."

Jenny then said, "Good, thank you. That could be a big help after closing all of my operations in Hong Kong. That's where my father and grandfather and my late husband actually started the business, almost fifty years ago. It was very hard for me to close up our operations there.

"Right now, we have everything relocated to Singapore.. Although my father and my father-in-law of my first husband moved to Singapore, it's not as easy to work with our European customers from Singapore as it was from Hong Kong. They have very different laws to work with in Singapore and many more restrictions on storage and shipping."

"So, frankly, I decided that I was going to set up a European operation, either in the UK or in Amsterdam. I know many folks in Amsterdam speak English, but I think I would be happier to have my company based here in London."

Peter said, "Well, I think either place would work very well; however, I would think putting your operation in the UK would be a great advantage for working with most of the countries, As you know. The British have had a very large influence in business throughout Europe for hundreds of years."

Jenny replied, "Well, I believe we agree on that. The question is do you think you could help me find a good warehouse to set up my operation that's not far out of London, has good access to ports, air and rail service?"

"As you may know, I'm not into renting warehouses, but I think I may know someone that can help you find what you are looking for."

"That would be great, could I ask you to contact your man for me?"

"Certainly, that's not a problem., However, my man isn't a man, but a woman who works with real estate that's both for sale and lease,"

"Thank you, that would be great."

"OK, I'll give her a call right now,"

After saying that, Peter took out his cell phone and placed a call.

The telephone call was soon answered and Peter said, "Hi, this is Peter Valkovich, May I speak with Wanda Jones, please?"

A few seconds later, Peter heard, "Good afternoon, Peter, this is Wanda."

"Hi, Wanda, I have a couple of people that I'm having lunch with that are looking for a large warehouse with good access to port, air and rail service. Do you know of anything that's available at this time?"

"Yes, Peter. I know of a couple of warehouses that would fit that bill. They are good buildings and they have great access to rail, air and sea operations,"

"Good, would you have time to show them to my friends this afternoon?"

"Sure, where do you want me to meet you or would you like for me to pick you up somewhere?

"I think it would be best if you picked us up, there are three of us."

"Great, where are you?"

"We are at the Claridge Hotel,"

"Peter, did you move back there again?"

"No, that's where my friends are staying,"

"OK, I'll pick you and your friends up in about thirty minutes,"

"Ok, we'll see you soon. We will be in the dining room. If you get here soon enough, maybe you could join us for lunch."

"OK, I'll do that. I'll be on my way as soon as I hang up my phone,"

Peter closed his cell phone, placed it back in a small cell phone holster on his belt and said, "She said she would join us for lunch."

Jenny replied, "That's good. I would enjoy having the opportunity to visit with her before we spend time looking at the property she has. I would like for her to tell us about the property, so I have an idea if what she has will work for our needs. There is no use wasting her time or ours if I don't think the property will meet our needs."

They continued talking and enjoying a glass of wine while waiting for Wanda Baxter to join them for lunch.

Almost exactly thirty minutes later, Wanda joined them at their table for lunch.

After a quick round of introductions, the waiter brought back a fourth chair and set up glasses and silverware for Wanda.

A short time later, they all gave the waiter their lunch orders.

Wanda was able to tell Jenny about the new port and warehouses being built just northeast of London. Jenny believed that what Wanda told her sounded like just what she needed to be able to set up her new European operations.

Not long after that, they were served their lunch and quickly finished it and were ready to take a trip to see this new port area.

CHAPTER EIGHT

CHECKING OUT BUSINESS PROPERTY

The four of them finished lunch and Peter said, "I have another meeting to go to, but I know you are in good hands. So, I will excuse myself and let Wanda help you."

Wanda said, "If it's all right, I will just take my car and let your driver follow me. We will be going to DP World London Gateway, it's located on the north bank of the River Thames. It's about thirty miles east of Central London. I think you will like this location. It offers you great access to most of the world since this port it linked weekly to fifty-one countries. Plus, they are building several new warehouses that could be available to buy or lease near the port."

Jenny said, "I think before you get started, since it's that far from where we are, maybe you should talk with our driver to make sure we don't lose you in all of this London traffic."

Wanda replied, "That's a good idea."

The four of them left the hotel and Benny pulled the Rolls up to pick up Tom and Jenny.

Benny got out of the Rolls and went to open the door for Jenny and Tom.

Tom turned to Wanda and said, "Wanda, this is our driver Benny. Would you please explain to Benny where we are going and how he can follow you in case we lose you on the way?"

"Certainly."

Benny asked, "Yes, ma'am, where are we going?"

"We are going to the new DP World Gateway. It's on the north bank of the River Thames; we will be traveling up the M-25 to the junction A-13 to Gateway Park. It's about 30 miles."

"From there, I'll just wait for you and then you can just follow me so your folks can see the area of the port and the new warehouses being built to serve the port."

Benny replied, "Yes, ma'am. I will follow you and if I get cut off, I'll continue up the M25 until I see your car at the inters ection of the A-13."

"Fine, let's get started,"

Benny got behind the steering wheel of the Rolls as Wanda got into her car and he started the engine of the Rolls.

Wanda quickly pulled out of the hotel driveway in front of several cars and Benny had to wait for the traffic to clear before he could get the Rolls out on the street. That would be the last glimpse of Wanda's car they would see until they got to the turn-off at A-13.

Tom asked Jenny, "Well, what did you think of Wanda Baxter, do you think she's involved with Peter's other business?"

No, I don't think she has anything to do with our friends,"

Benny was soon on the M-25 and traffic was not too bad and he thought he was making good time.

Suddenly, two cars that he thought must be racing each other were quickly coming up closer to him at a very high rate of speed.

Then, one of the cars pulled up next to him and the other car was actually bumping into his back bumper.

Benny saw the man in the car next to him was putting down the window and then Benny saw him pointing a gun at him.

Benny slammed on his brakes and the car behind him slammed into the limo and then went into a ditch, turning over.

Then, Benny quickly turned the limo over to the outside lane and got behind the car that the man who had pointed a gun at Benny was in. He ran the limo into the back bumper.

The driver in the second card tried to move over to the inside lane but Benny kept the limo's bumper against the car and increased his speed, pushing the car to a higher speed. Then, Benny hit his brakes and the second car went into the ditch, hit a signpost and began burning.

Benny quickly regained his car's speed and left the scene of the two-car accident far behind them as quickly as he could.

Tom said, "Wow, Benny, I didn't know you were a stunt driver. Great job getting rid of those people."

Benny replied, "In my younger days, I used to do stunt driving for the movie people. That was when it was too risky to have the movie stars doing those kind of things."

Jenny said, "Well, Benny, you've got a job with my company for the rest of your life because I'm pretty sure you certainly saved our lives."

"Thank you, Jenny."

Tom replied, "No, thank you, Benny!"

Several minutes later they arrived at the exit off of the M-25 and turned onto the A-13 and they saw Wanda waiting in her car.

Wanda started her car's engine and gave a wave to Benny to follow her and they were off to see the DP World London Gateway and the new warehouses and offices being constructed there.

Arriving at the port docks, Wanda found parking places for their cars, parked and got out of her car. Benny parked the limo next to her car.

When they all got out of their vehicles, Wanda asked, "You didn't have any problem following my direction, I guess, because I didn't have to wait very long before you arrived."

Tom replied, "No, Wanda, the directions you gave Benny were perfect. Plus, Benny is an outstanding driver and can handle about anything that comes at him."

As the three of them were walking away, Benny was checking over the damage to the Rolls. It was much less than he thought it would be, but it was still quite a bit for a brand-new Rolls Royce that was less than two weeks old. The front and back bumpers would need to be totally replaced. They were really smashed in, but he knew the other two cars were totaled.

He did wonder about the occupants in those two vehicles, were they badly hurt or dead?

He knew which way he hoped. Yeah, he hoped they were dead so they wouldn't be coming after his people again.

Wanda was a very good sales agent. She showed Tom and Jenny the docks and the new loading and unloading equipment that was in operation and which would cut the cost for handling the freight.

They had an opportunity to talk with some of the dock hands and their supervisors and everyone they met and talked to only had glowing things to say about the operations at the port.

Jenny was very impressed and knew her company could operate from this port very well.

After spending almost three hours talking with people at the docks and watching ships being loaded and unloaded, Wanda said, "Now, I want to show you the new warehouses that are in operation and some that are being built if you think you have seen enough of the operations at the port?"

Jenny replied, "Yes, thank you and I must say I'm very impressed with the port and the new loading and unloading equipment. It's the best I've ever seen."

"Good, then let's take a drive around some of the warehouses that are in operation and some that are still under construction so you will have a full understanding of how much the location can offer your company."

The three of them returned to their cars and Wanda said, "I'll just drive you around in my car so I can tell you about some of the companies that are now operating in our new port."

Jenny replied, "OK, that sounds good to me, Wanda."

Wanda drove them around several very new-looking warehouses that were now occupied and several other buildings that were still under construction. Again, Jenny was impressed and told Wanda she that was and would certainly consider moving some of her operations here,

Wanda assured her that when she was ready to move forward, she could help her with everything Jenny needed to get her business up and running in the UK.

Wanda drove them back to the Rolls and dropped them off. Jenny thanked her again for taking the time to show them the new port, and said that when she decided for sure to establish her European operation in England, she would contact her and work with her.

That pleased Wanda and she told Jenny, "If you can think of anything else I can do to help you make your decision, please let me know. I'm always available for my clients.

Wanda gave Jenny her business card and told Jenny to just give her a call and she would meet with her any time, said good-bye and headed back to London.

Wanda never said a word about their Rolls' bent-up bumpers. Perhaps she never noticed them or she was just too busy selling the port to Jenny. Guess they might never know which one it was.

Benny opened the door for Jenny and she got into the Rolls. Tom went around the other side of the car and Benny hurried to get Mr. Tom's door open for him even as Tom was telling Benny, "It's OK, you don't have to open and close the door for me."

Benny reply, "Yes, sir, Mr. Tom, I have to open and close the door for you and Miss Jenny."

"OK, Benny, you win,"

Their trip back to London was uneventful, not one car tried to run them off the road or shoot at them.

However, they did pass a couple of wrecked cars that were being loaded up on their way back to the center of London.

Later that night, the news on the Telly, as the British call the television, said there were four people killed in auto wrecks on the M-25 and the accidents were still under investigation.

The authorities thought these two cars had been racing and since they found weapons in the cars, the police thought they may have been rival gangs, The next day, Jenny had Benny take the Rolls back to the dealer and ask them to please obtain two new bumpers for the Rolls. Benny told the dealer that, apparently, some wild kids had a great time running some kind of old vehicle into the front and back bumpers of the Rolls when it was parked overnight.

The dealer called Jenny on her cell phone and explained that the bumpers are all handmade for each Rolls and it would be several months before they could get it repaired.

Jenny said, "What other color Rolls do you have in stock today to replace my silver one?"

"We do have a very beautiful blue one. We just put it on the showroom floor today."

Jenny said, "OK, I'll take the blue one and you can keep the silver one until you get the new bumpers put on it,"

"I'm sorry, but we can't just let you use the blue Rolls until we get the new bumpers made and installed on your silver Rolls."

I'm not talking about just using it. I'm talking about buying the blue Rolls, so I have a car to use today. Now do you understand?"

"Yes, Mrs, Parker. I certainly do understand."

"Good, tell me how much I owe you and I'll give you my American Express card number."

The manager told her the amount of the blue Rolls and she gave him her American Express number, and then she said, "You know, that's over a thousand pounds more than I paid a couple of weeks ago for the silver Rolls."

The sale manager said, "Yes, it is, Mrs. Parker, but our cost to build our cars is going up and it seems like it does it every day."

"OK, I can understand that, but just be sure you can get Benny on the way back to pick us up as quickly as you can."

"Yes, I will, Mrs. Parker and thank you again for your purchase,"

Tom asked, "What's the problem with getting the Rolls fixed?"

"They would have to make the bumpers so it's going to take several months before they can get it fixed."

"Fine, what are we going to do for a car?"

"I solved the problem, I bought another Rolls Royce."

"That figures, my darling Jenny, you know how to solve all the problems."

"Not quite, we don't know about the Prime Minister yet, do we?"

"Not yet, but we will."

CHAPTER NINE

WHAT'S GOING TO HAPPEN NEXT

Tom said, "Jenny, I'm not sure what we should do next. The only thing we know for sure is that ever since we've arrived in London it seems like we are the targets for somebody."

"At this point I'm not sure if it's the Russians or some terrorist group that recognized me from the past. The only thing we know for sure is whoever it is they are determined to kill me or us. I'm not sure if it's just me or both of us. Whoever it is they are really trying to get the job done."

Jenny replied, "Tom, you don't think it's the communist Chinese that's trying to kill me, because I moved all of my holdings out of Hong Kong, do you?"

"No, I don't think so, that's a little out of their standard operating procedures. They would have more likely found a way to keep you from taking your money and your people out of Hong Kong, rather than trying to kill you after you left the country with your people and your money."

"Well, I think I moved so fast they never realized what I was doing."

"Well, that was a good thing. I'm just sorry you lost so much money by moving so quickly."

"I'll make it back and my company and most of my key employees got out before it was too late."

Their thoughts were interrupted by Jenny's cell phone ringing.

Jenny answered her phone and she heard Peter say, "Good Morning, Jenny, this is Peter and I just wanted to know what you thought about what Wanda was able to show you yesterday."

"I was very impressed and I think DP World Gateway Port is perfect for what I'm looking for in Europe. I think it can be the perfect place to sit up my company's European Operation."

"That's great news. I'm sure Wanda will be pleased to hear that and I am certain you are making the right choice for a place to set up your European operation."

"Well, I was very impressed with the layout and the number of weekly links to fifty- one countries, that's great for my European Operation. I really appreciate your help, Peter."

"Jenny, I have a question for you."

"What's that Peter?"

"Would you consider hiring me as the Director for your European Operations?"

"Yes, I would, but I have to ask one question of you. I thought you were very successful with your own company's operations, so why would you consider working for me?"

"True, in the past I was very successful with my own company, but since the war in the Ukraine with Russia, things are not very good. Too many of my customers don't or can't do business with me because most of my products come from Russia. I can't import them anymore, so the truth is I really need a job to help me to keep up my life style."

"Peter, I would like to set up a meeting with you to discuss this if you really think you would be happy working for somebody else and not running your own company."

"Well, Jenny, I probably wouldn't be considering doing this if I hadn't had the chance of meeting you and Tom. But I really believe I could be an asset to your company and working with you would give me a real future. I don't know if you know it or not, but I've never lived in Russia. Plus, I'm certainly not happy about the things they are doing now."

"I do know that the Russian leaders don't represent the Russian people. The Russian people are decent and could be happy to live their lives in peace, but the leaders always want more and if they get it, then they will want more."

"OK, Peter, why don't we meet tomorrow for lunch at one and we will take the time to really discuss this idea of you joining my company."

"Great, Jenny! I'll see you tomorrow at your hotel for lunch and I'm really looking forward to telling you what I think I can do for you and your company in Europe."

Jenny replied, "OK, until tomorrow."

Jenny closed her phone and Tom asked, "So, what was that all about?"

"Not much, it seems Peter wants to run my European Operation for me."

Tom said, "He what?"

"Just what I said, Peter wants to come to work for me and run my European Operations."

"You've got to be kidding!"

"No, we are meeting him for lunch tomorrow at one at our hotel."

Well, that's about the last thing I would have ever thought about Peter asking you."

"Me, too."

"Jenny, I was so sure he was the one that was in charge of the people that have been trying to kill us and now he's asking you for a job. Unbelievable! Maybe he figures if he can't kill us, then he will go to work for you."

"I guess we will know more tomorrow, Tom."

Jenny opened her cell phone and called the hotel and set up a lunch reservation at the restaurant for three people at one pm.

The next morning Benny brought the blue Rolls and asked if they had any place they wanted to go this morning.

Jenny told him they would like him to take them on a short drive to see the two dock areas located south of London, but we have to be back by one o'clock for a lunch meeting at the Claridge Hotel.

Benny replied, "I'm sorry, ma'am, but I think it is too far and too much traffic to take you to see the Port of Southampton and the Port of Felixstowe, then get you back to the Claridge Hotel for your one o'clock lunch meeting."

Jenny asked, "Are you sure, Benny? It doesn't look like that far on the map"

"Yes, ma'am, I'm very sure. I would certainly be happy to take you there, but we could never get back through the traffic to the Claridge Hotel for your lunch meeting at one o'clock."

"OK, Benny, you know much better than I do. So, we will go to lunch and then after lunch we can go to see those two ports."

"Yes, ma'am."

"How long will it take us to get back to the hotel from here?"

"About an hour, maybe a little more than an hour."

"My, the traffic in London is really slow, isn't it?"

"Yes, ma'am, it's a very old city with a lots of people trying to go to a lot of different places."

"Thank you, Benny, I' ll try to remember that. So, just go into our kitchen and have some tea and biscuits."

"Thank you, ma'am."

CHAPTER TEN

LUNCH MEETING
WITH PETER

About ten-thirty, Jenny told Benny they were ready to go to the Claridge Hotel.

The three of them were soon in the blue Rolls and. true to his word. Benny had them at the Claridge Hotel just a few minutes past an hour.

Jenny and Tom went into the hotel and went directly to their suite on the top floor of the hotel. They were in their suite by eleven forty-five and they had been there only a few minutes before the room telephone rang.

Tom picked up a phone and said, "Tom Parker."

The caller said "Is this the famous CIA Agent, Tom Parker?"

Tom replied, "I don't know if I'm a famous CIA Agent, but I'm Tom Parker."

The voice of the phone said, "I'm looking forward to killing the CIA's top agent."

Tom said, "I hope you brought help, because I think you're going to need it. You're not doing very well so far."

The voice said, "Oh, I won't need it. I've got my own way of doing things, but I promise you, you'll know when it's coming."

The phone went dead.

Jenny asked, "Who was that on the phone?"

"The man who is going to kill me."

"What?"

"I just told you what the man on the telephone told me. He said he was going to kill me and I would know when it was coming."

"Tom, I think we better go home. This whole thing is getting really weird."

"Yes, everything about this trip is weird. We are here to check out if Peter Valkovich is trying to get the British Prime Minister to help the Russians against America just because he and his wife were guests of this Russian business man going to see a couple of ballets and now this same Russian business man is trying to get you to hire him to run your European Operation."

"Plus, we have had people trying to kill us ever since we got to London and they don't seem to understand that we are here just to make sure the Prime Minster is still on our side. Weird is not even the right word for this whole situation. It's nuts!"

"Tom, you must have had things like this happen to you when your worked full time for the CIA."

"Oh, I had lots of people trying to kill me, but they hardly ever called me on the phone to tell me they were going to kill me, like never!"

"So, what do you want to do, Tom?"

"Well, the first thing we need to do is go down to the restaurant to meet Peter and see if I can live long enough to have lunch."

"Tom, please quit saying that. It's making me tremble, just the thought of it. I've already lost a husband and I'll be damned if I'm going to lose you."

"OK, my love. Let's calm down and go down to meet Peter for lunch and to see if I actually get to eat my lunch before this guy kills me."

"Tom, please don't say that!"

"OK, no more jokes about him killing me before lunch."

"Good, lets hear what Peter has to say about coming to work for me."

Tom and Jenny made sure they closed and locked the door of the suite and Tom placed a very small magnet on the bottom of the door lever. He positioned it so that if a person grasped the door handle, the magnet would either fall off or be moved from its original position.

They made their way to an elevator and quickly got on to take them down to the floor where their restaurant was located.

They were soon in the restaurant and the maitre d', Charles, recognized Jenny and Tom and said, "Madam Parker, how are you today?"

Jenny replied, "We're just fine and we are looking forward to a very nice lunch."

He replied, "Well, I certainly hope we meet your expectations and serve you a wonderful lunch."

"I'm sure you will, everything we have had here has been wonderful."

"Thank you, I believe you have a table reserved for three, is that correct?"

"Yes, it is, Mr. Peter Valkovich will be joining us."

"Very good, we are always happy to see Mr. Peter. You know he lived in the hotel for a long time and all our staff has a special place in our heart for him. He's such a wonderful gentleman."

"Yes, we believe he is."

Charles showed them to their special table in the back of the restaurant near the back wall. There, they could talk without being disturbed by other diners.

Tom and Jenny had only been seated a short while before Peter joined them.

Jenny said, "You know, Peter. I was very surprised, but pleased, that you maybe interested in working as my Director of European Operations."

"Frankly, Jenny, I maybe as surprised as you are about that, but I think I need to join a company like yours that doesn't just depend on one country for all their products. Plus you have a wonderful company with quality products and a great reputation for how your company deals with your customers and your employees."

"That's very nice to hear, Peter. I know we haven't been very active in the European market, but we do have several large accounts already established in the UK, France and Germany."

"Well, Jenny. I did know your company had been very successful with several companies in Europe, but I think by setting up operations here in the UK, you will be shocked to see how large and how fast your European market will expand. Your company is not exactly the new kid in the market here in Europe, but I think you have as the American's like to say, just the tip of the iceberg, or something like that."

Tom and Jenny laughed and Jenny said, "Oh, God, I hope it's not an iceberg, they sink ships."

That brought a big smile to Peter's face and he said, "I know that Suri Pearson never likes hearing anything about any sinking ships because any time a big ship sinks it costs her family big money."

Jenny asked, "How's that, Peter?"

"Well, her family has a big stake in Lloyd's of London. You know, the company that insures virtually ever ship that carries cargo anywhere in the world? Her dad is the President of Lloyd's of London and their family is the one of the largest stockholders in the company."

Tom said, "Well, I guess if I were a member of that family. I wouldn't like hearing about any ship sinking either."

Peter replied, "Well, if you had any idea of how much money that company is worth. Maybe, you wouldn't get too worried."

Jenny said, "I see our waiter standing a little way back from our table and he seems ready to take our orders. Maybe, we should order our lunch and talk more after we get our orders in."

Tom replied, "Yes. dear, I think you're right."

Then Tom motioned to the waiter to come over to their table and he said, "Yes, waiter, we are ready for you to take our lunch orders."

The waiter took their orders and headed to the kitchen to give their orders to the kitchen staff.

Jenny asked, "Peter, I know you are aware of the ports that serve the London area; which port would you think would be the best to serve my company's needs?"

"Well, of course almost everyone in the world knows or has heard about the Port of Southampton that has served the London area for many years. However, I think we would be better served if we set up our operations at the new port, DP World London Gateway."

"Why would you say that, Peter?"

"Jenny, in the first place it is all very new with the latest loading and unloading equipment, plus the warehouses are all new and with many more being built at this time. Also, I believe housing for our staff would be newer and maybe a little less costly for your employees. Plus, traffic will be much easier to get in and out of the port with fewer delays."

"Peter, I haven't see the two big ports located south of London, Felixstowe and Southampton, but since our driver Benny told me it would take more than hour to get there, I think you are probably right. The new port is probably the best choice for us."

"Jenny, I'm sure you are right and since Wanda picked DP World London Gateway Port to show you over the south ports, this lady knows her real estate and what would be your best buy and what she believes would work the best for your company."

"OK, Peter, I think that's where we should plan our headquarters for our European operation. Can you think of any reason that we shouldn't pick that location?"

"Only one."

"What's that, Peter?"

"I'm going to need to sell my house in the south part of London, but the way the price of real estate keeps going up. I will probably make a nice profit by selling my home now."

Jenny and Tom had to laugh at that small problem poor Peter would have.

Perfect timing. The waiter arrived with their lunch.

The three of them turned their attention to their lunch and the conversation dwindled down.

After they had finished their lunch, Jenny asked Peter about what type of salary do you need to come to work with my company full-time?

Peter thought for a few seconds and said, "I would need a salary of two hundred fifty thousand Pounds a year, plus travel expenses and a small percentage of the profits that I can help you make ever year."

Jenny replied, "That salary will work for me, plus, I will give you two percent of the yearly profits from all sales made in Europe."

Peter asked, "Would that include the business customers you already have in Europe?"

"Yes, it would. If it's a sale in Europe you will get your percentage of the profit. It will make our bookkeeping easier.

Tom asked, "Peter, do you think your association with the British Prime Minster has helped you in business?"

"Strange you would ask that, but I certainly think it helps me here in England.

However, our friendship really has nothing to do with my business. The truth is, Blake and I just hit it off from the first time we met and I love his wife Suri. I certainly enjoy spending time with both of them."

Tom said, "Is there something that makes you think Blake and Suri enjoy being with you so much? I've heard you have even treated them to a couple of trips to attend ballets in Paris and Moscow."

"Tom, you may not know Suri was an up and coming ballet star until she was injured and then could no longer perform, but she still loves the ballet. So, I take them for that reason, I buy their tickets. However, Blake always pays for the transportation, meals, hotels, and the government pays for their security force and his man Hanson to travel with us."

"Peter, did you know that people always thought that you were paying for everything for these trips when you went with him and Suri?"

"No, but I can tell you Blake would never accept that from anyone. He's always been the one to pay for everything for him and his friends.

"It was hard enough for him to ever agree to let me pay for the tickets for the ballets. Blake was so used to always paying for everything that he or his friends ever wanted to do. He was always the man with the money in his hands, always ready to pay for anything he or they wanted to do."

Tom said, "If you two will please excuse me, I need to take a trip to the men's room."

Jenny replied, "OK, Tom. I think I need to have a little more time to visit with Peter to get the timing set up for him to start working as my European Director of Operations."

Tom got up and left to find the nearest men's toilet.

Tom was told he would have to go to the front of the restaurant for the closest one. Tom walked to the front of the restaurant and found the men's toilet. Tom went inside and headed to a urinal near the back of the room.

Just as he approached the urinal, suddenly the lights went off and he heard a man say, "I told you that you would know it when you were about to die."

Tom immediately dropped to the floor and rolled to his left toward an enclosed toilet stool section that he had remembered seeing when he came into the men's room.

Getting there, he managed to quickly pull himself under the metal wall. He put the toilet seat and cover down over the toilet. Then he managed to stand up on the toilet cover and look over the wall in the dark room.

He saw the man who had threatened him approaching the toilet booth with a flashlight pointing to the floor of the booth Tom was in.

Just as the man leaned down to try to see under the booth to locate Tom, Tom leaped from the toilet with both of his hands held flat to hit the toilet door, making the door swing open. The door hit the killer with Tom's full weight and strength, sending the man reeling across the toilet floor.

As he was falling to the floor, his flashlight fell out of his left hand and a large knife fell from his right hand.

Just then someone opened the men's room door and flipped on the lights. The man just stood there when he saw a man laying on the floor and another man picking up a large knife and placing the knife in the sink. Next, the man that put the knife in the sink grabbed the man on the floor and began choking the man who was trying to get up and was wildly swinging his fist at the man who was choking him.

Suddenly, the man who was choking the other man took his hands off of the man's neck and gave him two quick karate chops on his throat and down the man went and was out.

Next, the man who knocked out the other man reached down and took off the man's belt and quickly pulled his hands behind his back and secured his hands with the man's belt.

Then, Tom calmly said, "Would you be so kind to get someone who works at the restaurant and ask them to call the police and have them come back to the restroom to get this man who tried to kill me with that big knife."

"Yes, sir, I'll go right now and get someone."

The man who had been waiting to come into the men's went running down the hallway screaming, "Call the police! Some man tried to kill another man in here."

Very soon, the head waiter came into the men's room followed by a hotel security officer along with Jenny and Peter.

Jenny asked, "Are you all right, Tom?"

"Yes, love, but no thanks to the man lying on the floor. He tried to kill me with that big knife in the sink."

By that time, several police officers arrived at the scene and Lieutenant Johnson asked Tom, "Is this the man who tried to kill you with that knife?"

"Yes, Lieutenant, that's the man."

"What's you name, sir?"

"General Tom Parker and I'm with the CIA on a special mission for the President of the United States."

Tom opened up his documents and handed them to Lieutenant Johnson.

The Lieutenant looked over Tom's official CIA documents and said, "Thank you, General Parker, I recognize this man. He's wanted on several charges for a lot of different crimes, including murder. You did a service for England. I will have to ask you to stop by Scotland Yards and fill out a complaint form before you leave London."

"Yes, sir, I will be happy to do that if it will help keep this man off the streets of London."

Jenny said, "Tom, I think we better take a little time before we do much else today."

Peter said, "I think that's a good idea and it will give me some time to make some contacts to check out some of your products. I'm sure many of my customers will find things you have on your company's website that they can use. Plus, it will give them a better idea of all of your products."

"Good idea ,Peter. I' 11 give you a call in the morning and we can set up a meeting sometime tomorrow."

CHAPTER ELEVEN

THE BIG QUESTION IS WHO SENT THIS MAN

Tom told Jenny, "I think we better make a stop in our suite before we leave the hotel. I never got to use the toilet before I was attacked, and I'm feeling very uncomfortable now."

Jenny agreed and they went up to their suite so Tom would have the opportunity to use the bathroom without anyone trying to kill him, he hoped.

Tom checked before they went into the suite to see if his little door device had been moved. It hadn't and this made Tom feel more comfortable.

Their suite was safe and Tom made his way into the bathroom and took care of a pressing problem. He was soon out of the bathroom and asked Jenny, "So, who do you think is behind all the problems that we've had since we arrived in London?"

"Somehow, I'm having a hard time believing that it's Blake Pearson, and now, I don't think it's Peter, not after we've spend so much time with him."

"No, Jenny, I doubt that Peter is the one behind the men who have been attacking me or us. I'm somehow overlooking the person who's behind these attacks."

"Tom, do you think it might be someone who works for Blake Pearson that could have some kind of ties with the Russians?"

"Probably not, Jenny, but we can't rule anyone out. I even wonder about Blake's stepbrother, you know, Hanson Churchill?"

Jenny replied, "Well he certainly knows everything that's going on with Prime Minster Pearson."

"You're right, Jenny, he seems to be with Blake Pearson almost all the time, even on the ballet trips. I wonder if he even has a girl friend or even has a life of his own. I'm going to see what our people with the CIA here in London know about what kind of a life he has when he's not with Blake Pearson."

Tom got his cell phone and called the London CIA office and asked to speak with Robert Clark.

The operator could see that it was Tom Parker calling and put his call through to Robert Clark's phone.

Only a few seconds passed and Tom heard, "This is Robert Clark, how can I help you, Tom?"

"I have a question for you about Hanson Churchill. How much does the agency know about him?"

"Well, we know a lot about him. As you already know, he's like a kid brother to Blake Pearson. He was raised along with Blake by the Pearson's after Hanson's parents were killed in a car accident while working for the Pearsons. He is only a few months younger than Blake and Hanson got all of the same benefits growing up as Blake did."

"The Pearson's treated him as if he was one of their own children. They adopted him but let him keep his family's name, since Churchill is a pretty famous name in England. He got a college degree, cars,and clothes, the same as Blake. He wasn't quite as good of a scholar as Blake, but he was good enough to earn a law degree."

Tom asked, "How about vices? You know, like girls, gambling or drugs?"

"Well, if he does, we have no information about any of those. He's had several girl friends, but no big problems with any of them. He's currently dating a young widow with a three or four year old boy."

"What happened to the young woman's husband?"

"He died of a heart attack while giving a speech to some young church group. He was a minster for the church and he was teaching a class at that time."

"Is there anything suspicious about his death?"

"No, he had heart problems for several years, although he was pretty young to die like that since he was only in his thirties."

"What do you know about the girlfriend?"

"She's also in her thirties and she is a daughter of a minster and his wife, both of her parents have a religious education."

"Her mother has served as a missionary in Africa ,working to help various tribes get access to water, and teaching women about using sanitary pads for their periods. Before her, the women were thought to be unclean when they were having their periods. They had to stay away from the rest of the tribe as long as they were bleeding and had to stay in a special tent away from their husband and children."

"In other words, they had to stay away from the rest of the tribe until their period was over. Then they were thought to be clean, so they could come back and live with the rest of the tribe."

"She then taught some of the women in the tribe to actually be able to make pads for the women in her tribe from material they had available to them and they began selling them to women in other tribes and taught them how to use them."

"Sounds like her mother was a very sharp missionary to be able to help get water so their tribe didn't have to keep moving all of the time to find water, and she certainly changed the life of all of the women in the tribe."

"Yes, she was and she helped to get some Americans to help the tribe to find water and to drill a well to keep the water flowing year around for the tribe. The Americans even built a water tower to store their water."

"I would have to think the daughter was a pretty solid citizen with her background."

"No doubt that she is, Tom, and she would be a solid foundation for someone like Hanson Churchill."

"Do you know how long they have been going together?"

"The best information we have, it's almost a year."

"It sounds like Hanson likes her a lot."

"Well, we think so; it's the longest relationship he's ever had with any woman that we know of."

"Robert, I can't figure out who has so much information about every move I make in London and then keep having people trying to kill me, do you have any idea?"

"No, we've had a meeting here in my office trying to figure that one out and we can't come up with the answer to that question."

Well, Robert, I'm sure as hell can't figure it out and if they keep trying like they have been, I'm afraid one of them will be successful before I can kill them."

"I don't believe that, none of them have had much luck so far, and from what I've heard about your life, no one has ever come close to doing that."

"Well, that's true, but I've never been in a place that I couldn't tell the bad guys from the good guys like it has been here in London. I guess the best thing I can do is just handle it like I've had to do it in the past, consider everyone I meet as a potential threat to mine and Jenny's life."

"Well, that's worked pretty well for you for a lot of years, Tom, so I would recommend you just keep doing it."

"Damn right, that's what I'm going to do."

CHAPTER TWELVE

JUST KEEP DOING IT LIKE YOU'VE BEEN DOING IT

Tom told Jenny, "Well, Robert Clark doesn't have any better idea who's behind the people that are trying to kill us than we do. So, he's not a lot of help."

"Seriously, did you really think he would have any better idea who's behind all of the people who have been trying to kill us since we been here, than we did?"

"Well, I could only hope, especially since he is the CIA Agent in charge of the London office. He should have a better pulse on what's going on here than we do."

"Tom, they never had this problem in London before we came here. London didn't have Tom Parker, famous CIA Agent who saves the President of the United States of America and the rest of the world."

"Jenny, I've never saved the President."

"Well, you've saved everybody else."

"Not quite everybody, but I've tried. How about a big kiss and let's change the subject and think of a much better things to do."

"Do you have a better idea?"

"Yes," as he pulled Jenny into his arms and gave her a big kiss and ran his right hand up under her skirt and found just where he wanted it to be.

Sometime later Jenny said, "I think we should get dressed and see if we can spend the rest of the day thinking about who could be behind all of the attempts that have been made trying to kill us since we arrived in London."

"I don't know, Jenny, but I think I had a much better idea earlier."

"Yes, my dear, you did, but I think you might not be up to a repeat performance right now."

"Damn, I hate it when you are right about something,, especially about this something."

Tom began finding his clothes and picking up Jenny's clothes and handing them to her. They were soon dressed and on their way back to CIA London Headquarters.

Tom locked up their suite again and he and Jenny went down to the main floor of the Claridge Hotel and found their driver Benny who had been sitting visiting with several other drivers.

Seeing them, he bid his friends goodbye and said, "Is everything OK and are you ready to go, Tom?"

"Thank you, Benny, we are really ready to go."

Benny said, "Well, your car is sitting just a little way from the front door. Would you like for me to pull it up to the door so you can get in?"

Jenny saw where their car was parked and replied, "No, that's not necessary, we can walk that far."

Benny hurried ahead of them and quickly opened the right rear door of the limo and Jenny got into the car.

Tom was walking around to the back of the limo to get into the car on the left side, when suddenly Tom saw a small black car come right at him, going way too fast through this driveway.

Tom quickly dove toward the left back side of the limo and fell to the pavement. The driver of the little black car was out of the driveway into the street and was soon out of sight.

Benny saw what happened and rushed around to the back left side of the limo to be sure Tom was OK.

When Benny got to where Tom was laying, he asked, "Mr. Tom, are you OK? I thought that car was going to hit you."

"I'm OK, but whoever was driving that little black car certainly was trying his best to hit me."

"I'm so sorry, Mr. Tom, from now on. I'm pulling the limo up to the door to pick up you and Miss Jenny."

"Thank you, Benny. I guess you will have to do that because, apparently, every one in London has the job of trying to kill me. Can you give me a hand and help me up so I can get in the backseat with Jenny?"

"I'm so sorry, sir."

Benny reached his hand down and Tom grabbed his hand and Benny helped to pull Tom up. Then, Benny opened the door and Tom got into the limo.

Jenny asked, "What was that all about?"

"Someone in that little black car just tried to run me down as I was going around the back of the limo. I jumped down onto the pavement on the back left side of the limo to keep them from hitting me."

"Thank God, you are all right."

"Well, I'm pretty good, except for the bleeding on my hands and knees, and my pants are pretty greased up from the oil leaking from some of the cars that had parked there."

Jenny said, "Let me see your hands."

Tom showed her his hands which were pretty scratched up and bleeding. Then Jenny said, "Pull your pant legs up so I can see your knees."

Tom did as she asked and after Tom pulled up his pant legs up she could see his knees were bleeding worse than his hands.

After seeing both of his hands and knees, she said, "I think when we get to CIA's headquarters we need to have someone take a look at your wounds and get you some meds to help stop the bleeding."

"Tom, you also are going to have to have some new pants to wear. These look like the ones the little boys who have been down on their knees playing all day, running their cars and wearing holes in the knees of their pants."

Tom quickly replied, "I promise. I won't do it again, mommy."

"Well, I'm not your mother and if I were, you sure wouldn't be a CIA Agent."

When they arrived at the CIA building, Benny drove the limo up to the floor where Tom and Jenny's apartment was located . After they were safely in their apartment,

Tom called Robert Clark and told him, "Someone in a small black car just tried to run over me while I was walking around the back of the car at the hotel to get in on the left side on the limo."

"Are you all right, Tom?"

"I'm OK. I just had to really hurry to get around the back of the limo before that little black car hit me. Believe me, he was trying his best, his best just wasn't quite good enough."

Robert said, "I'm sorry, what can we do?"

Tom replied, "I need someone to help me stop the bleeding on my hands and knees and put some bandages on my wounds."

After about ten minutes, Robert came up to the apartment to check on them.

Robert brought a woman that worked in the office with him that did some cleaning and helping with anything for someone who needed help.

Robert introduced her to Tom and Jenny and said, " Mary is the go-to person in the office who takes care of everything that no one else knows how to do."

Mary replied, "Yes, I'm the mother to the rest of this helpless staff that works in this office, so let me take a look at your wounds and I'll see if I can take care of you."

Tom quickly pulled up his pant legs and showed her his knees and held his hands up so she could see both of them. Mary said, "First thing, go ahead and pull those pants off so I can get those knees cleaned up, they look a lot worse than your hands."

Tom kind of hesitated taking his pants off.

Then Mary said, "You don't have anything under those pants that I haven't seen before, after raising four boys and working as a nurse's aide in an army hospital."

Tom replied, "No, I guess I don't." As Tom unfastened his belt and stood up letting his pants fall down around his feet, Mary quickly pulled his shoes, socks and pants off and handed his pants to Jenny and said, "These pants don't look like they can be saved, might as well put them in the trash bin."

Jenny replied, "Yes, Mary. I think you're right and she dropped them in a trash bin."

Then Mary cleaned the blood off Tom's knees and put medicine on them to keep them from becoming infected and placed bandages on both knees. Next, she did the same to Tom's palms, but didn't put any bandages on the wounds.

Mary said, "I don't think it would do much good to put a bandage on your palms because every time you opened or closed your hands, they would be popping off, so I put a couple of small round Band Aids right in the center of your palms to help stop the bleeding and let the wounds heal quicker."

Tom said, "Thank you, Mary, for taking care of my wounds."

Mary replied, "You must be one tough son-of -a -gun, you didn't even flinch when I put that antiseptic on those wounds."

Jenny quickly said, "Oh, he is one tough son-of -a -gun, but I really think he just can't feel pain any more. He's been wounded so many times before."

Tom replied to Jenny's statement, "I do hope you two ladies will just not talk about my ability to withstand pain, so I can just go into the bathroom and cry all by myself."

Both women just laughed at Tom's statement.

Mary then replied, "OK, CIA Agent Tom Parker. I'll be on my way now, but I'll be back to help you when the next bad guy actually gets to hit you with his car."

Tom replied, "Don't worry, Mary, next time I'll just pull my weapon and shoot them."

Mary retorted, "Sounds like a good idea, let somebody else's mother take care of them." That made all of them laugh, including, Mary.

CHAPTER THIRTEEN

TODAY THE PLOT
BECOMES VERY FOGGY

Jenny made coffee and found someone had brought some very nice -looking cinnamon rolls to their apartment.

When Robert arrived, Jenny suggested they sit around the kitchen table and partake of some coffee and cinnamon rolls. She asked Benny to join them and she had no trouble with the four of them sitting around the table and the men eating the cinnamon rolls and drinking their coffee.

Tom, Benny and Robert were happy to enjoy the cinnamon rolls and the coffee Jenny made for them.

Tom and Robert were talking about the latest attempt on Tom's life as he was leaving the hotel, which had occurred right in the hotel's front entrance.

Robert said, "It's almost unbelievable, how could someone know exactly when you were leaving the hotel and position the car to run you down like that."

Benny said, "The only way would be that someone in the hotel called the man in the little black car when Mr. Tom was coming out of the front door of the hotel."

Tom said, "You know I think Benny is right about that. I actually never even thought about that. We need to have someone talk to the folks working in the hotel about it."

Robert replied, "I'll have some of my people talk to the folks that were working in the hotel at that time to see if we can find out who would have called someone as you were leaving the hotel."

Tom replied, "I think that's a good idea. Maybe they could find out who made that call and who they were calling."

Robert left the apartment and met with three of his people and told them about this morning's attempt on Tom's life at the hotel.

Then three CIA men left their headquarters and drove to the hotel to question as many people who worked at the hotel that might have made such a call or saw someone in the lobby at that time making a call.

Arriving at the hotel they begin talking with all of the employees that had been working at the same time as Tom and Jenny were leaving the hotel.

After questioning all of the employees, the Bell Captain, the man in charge of the bellmen told them that a young woman a real "looker" approached him and told him she was doing a story for the Daily Mail, about one of the richest women in the world that was staying at the hotel, Jenny Parker.

The young woman told him that Jenny agreed to do the interview, but Jenny didn't want her to take her picture because, she didn't want people to know what she looked like.

The woman told the man that her editor insisted that he couldn't pay her for the interview if she didn't have a picture of the woman to go with the interview.

So the woman said, "I've got to have a picture of her to go with my interview or I won't get paid."

The man said he asked the young woman, what she wanted him to do to help her. He said the woman said if you would just call me on my cell phone. I'11 be waiting with my photographer at the front of the hotel, so when she's leaving the hotel he can take her picture.

He added that the woman said, "I'll give you a hundred pounds if you just call this number and I'll know when she's leaving the hotel and then I'll get her picture for my story."

The CIA Agent asked, "Did you call the cell number when Jenny was leaving the hotel?"

"Yes, I did."

"Did she pay you the hundred pounds after you called her?"

"No, she paid me after she talked to me about calling her, she said she trusted me that if I said I'd call, then I would."

The Agent asked, "Did you talk with the young woman when you made the call?"

"No."

"Do you still have the cell number you were to call?"

"No, I threw it away."

"Where did you throw it away?"

"In this trash bin."

"Please look to see if it's still there."

The Bell Captain picked up the trash bin and found the paper with the number on it and handed it to the CIA Agent. The Bell Captain said, "I'm sorry. I didn't know that taking this lady's picture was such a big deal."

The Agent replied, "No, taking her picture wasn't, but trying to run down one of our Agents is, they were trying to kill one of our CIA Agents, who's traveling with Jenny Parker."

The Agents searched the area and found the discarded cell phone in a bush around the comer where the little black car had apparently been parked.

As the Agents were leaving the hotel the Bell Captain asked, "Would a picture of the young woman be of any help?"

The CIA Agent that had been talking to him replied, "It certainly would, and do you have a picture of the young lady?"

The Bell Captain replied, "No, but I'm sure I can get you one from our security camera."

"Thank you; please see what you can do to get me the picture."

The Bell Captain invited the Agent to come with him behind the counter and into a small room behind where the Bell Captain's desk was located.

The Bell Captain stopped the camera from recording and began to roll back the film taken by his camera and after some time the Bell Captain stopped the film and said, "That's the young woman."

The CIA Agent said, "Well she a "looker" all right, and please print me a picture of her if you can."

"Yes, sir."

A few minutes passed and the Bell Captain handed him a picture of the young woman who asked him to call her when Jenny Parker was leaving the hotel lobby.

The CIA Agent thanked him and then, he along with the other CIA Agents, left the hotel and drove back to CIA Headquarters.

When they arrived back at their office, they met with Robert Clark and told him what they had found out about how the man in the little black car knew when Tom and Jenny were leaving the hotel.

Then they gave Robert the copy of the picture of the young woman who got the Bell Captain to call and let the man in the car know that Jenny and Tom where leaving the hotel. Then they gave him the cell phone that they found that the call had been made to.

They had already checked and found that some man from Denmark purchased the phone when he arrived in London and he had given the phone company cash for the purchase and one month's service. Now the phone service would end in fifteen days.

Robert looked over the young woman's picture and said, "Well, the Bell Captain's right, she's a "looker" that's for sure.

Robert contacted Scotland Yards and asked to speak with Captain Jack Hayes, and soon Captain Hayes answered his phone and said, "Captain Hayes, how may I help you?"

"Jack, it's Robert Clark with the CIA and I need a favor. One of my visiting CIA Agents by the name of Tom Parker was almost run over this morning leaving the Claridge Hotel."

"Robert, you Yanks never pay any attention to our traffic laws, no wonder he about got ran over."

"Yes, I know Jack, but he was just getting into a car in the driveway at the Claridge Hotel when some fellow in a small black car did his best to run over him."

"Robert, are you telling me he was *trying* to run over him?"

"Yes, that's what I'm telling you, and the only clue we have is that a young woman had paid the Bell Captain to call her when he and his wife were leaving the hotel."

"Which he did, then a small black car did its best to run over our Agent in the driveway of the Claridge. We have a copy of a picture of the young woman who paid the Bell Captain to call her when our agent was leaving the hotel. I wanted to see if you can ID her for us?"

OK, Robert, send me a copy of her picture and I'll see if we can ID her for you. When you have a chance to talk to me more, tell me how one of your Agents can afford to be staying at the Claridge Hotel."

"I didn't tell you that he was staying at the Claridge; however he and his wife are staying there. The clue to staying there is to marry one of the richest women in the world, that will work for you every time."

"Damn Yanks, you always find a way to live a lot better than us poor English cousins."

"Well, I guess you are just going to have to get rid of that King and get a lowly President to run your country like we do."

"You did say ruin your country like they do, didn't you?"

"OK, you win; some of them do a pretty good job of ruining the country."

"Send me the damn picture. I'll see if we can help you."

"Yes, sir." Robert hung up the phone and sent the picture.

Less than an hour later, Robert received a call back from Captain Hayes and he told Robert, "Well, you are in luck we found out the lady in the picture is a freelance reporter named Lucy Brown and the only police complaints about her are from agents and managers for TV and movie stars for harassing their stars for interviews and one for speeding, otherwise she got a clean record."

Robert asked Captain Hayes, "How about any information on boyfriends or relatives of Lucy?"

"Well, the only note that one of the officers that talked with her wrote said she had an uncle that works for Prime Minster Pearson in Security, some man by the name of Lawrence Sparks."

"Do you know anything about Mr. Sparks?'

"Not much, but what I do know is it's not Mr. Sparks, it's Colonel Sparks, he's the head of the Prime Minister's security detail. He's one of those people who keep pretty much out of the public view and there is little to nothing that the public would even know about the man."

"You mean, he like almost invisible to even Scotland Yard's?"

"Not quite, what we know is he has the highest security clearance of any person working in the Prime Minister's office and he is a retired Colonel from the Army Intelligent Department."

"Does he have a wife or family?"

"He's never married, except to the Army. He has a couple of sisters that he doesn't seem to have much or any contact with."

"Guess you knew more about him than you thought."

"Yes, we knew a little, but we know a lot more about you and the people you work with then we do about Colonel Sparks, that's for sure."

"I'm sure you do, he sounds like the kind of man that's all about England and less about himself and his family."

"You've got that right. I'm not sure if he even knew anything about a niece, much less would do anything to help her if she was in a jam with the police."

"Thanks for your help, Captain Hayes."

Robert called Tom and told him what Captain Hayes told him. The young woman was Lucy Brown, a freelance reporter, who gave the bell captain a hundred pounds to call when Jenny left the hotel.

Robert said he would check to see if they could find an address for Lucy Brown. It only took a few minutes before Robert called Tom back and told him he had an address for her.

Robert said, "I called a friend of mine, who works for The London Times, and he gave me her phone number and her address. Her cell phone number is 321-888-7777 and her address is 4875 Chelsea Ave London, UK."

Tom replied, "What took you so long? However, that's got to be the fastest anyone ever got me an address for someone that I was trying to find."

Robert replied, "You just have to know the right people to get information that quick. You have to have friends that are in the newspaper business."

"Great so give me the information."

Robert gave Tom, Lucy's telephone number and her address.

After Tom wrote down Lucy's telephone number and her address he called Benny and told him he wanted him to take him to Lucy's address to see if he could talk with her.

Benny met Tom with the Rolls and they were soon on their way to Lucy's address.

When they arrived at her address, Tom told Benny to wait in the car and he would see if Lucy was at home.

Tom walked across the street from where Benny parked the car and rang the doorbell.

Only a few seconds passed and Lucy opened her door and asked, "Yes, sir. Can I help you?"

Tom asked, "Are you Lucy Brown?"

She replied, "Yes, sir, how can I help you?

Tom replied, "Do you know who I am?"

"No sir, I have no idea who you are?"

Tom said, "Do you know you almost got me killed yesterday?"

"How did I almost get you killed? That's crazy."

Tom then asked, "Did you pay the bell captain one hundred pounds yesterday at the Claridge Hotel to call your cell phone when Jenny Parker was coming out of the Claridge Hotel?"

"I did."

"Why did you do that?"

"Because I had a photographer that was going to take her picture when she was came out of the hotel to get into her Rolls Royce. I needed her picture for an article about her for a newspaper story that I was writing."

"Did your photographer get her picture?"

"Yes, he did."

"Can I see the picture he took?"

"May I ask what does this has to do with you anyway?"

"I'm Jenny's husband. I'm Tom Parker and you almost got me killed yesterday."

"How in the hell did I almost get you killed?"

"I'll tell you how, because when the bell captain called your so-called photographer, a driver in a little black car did his best to try to run over me when I was coming out of the hotel, and if I hadn't jumped behind the Rolls I would have been."

Lucy took a careful look at Tom and said, "I think you better come into the house and spend some time talking with me about what really happened yesterday morning when you were coming out of the hotel."

Tom replied, "I think that would be a very good idea."

Lucy opened the door wider so Tom could come into her house.

When Tom was inside her house she asked him to sit down on a couch.

After Tom was seated, Lucy asked, "Why do you think this car was trying to run over you?"

Tom answer was guarded, "Perhaps, it was someone who doesn't want my wife to establish one of her companies here and they thought if they killed me maybe she wouldn't want to set up one of her companies here, I really don't know."

Lucy looked Tom straight into his eyes and said, "Don't you think it might be because you are some kind of a secret agent for the American Government?"

Tom looked Lucy straight into her eyes and said, "Maybe that's why someone tried to run me down."

Lucy replied, "It's pretty well known that Jenny Parker is married to a retired CIA Agent named Tom Parker. Your picture has been in the newspaper when the President was giving you another award for something you did."

"OK, you've got me. So tell me why you had to go to so much trouble to try to get a picture of Jenny?"

"Well, I heard that Jenny didn't like to have her picture in the newspaper. So I was going to get her picture to use with my article, and I hired my friend Steve Black to take her picture and he did and sent it to me."

"Lucy, have you known Steve a long time?"

"Yes, and for a while, I thought we were going to get married. He is one of the best photographers in the country, except when he goes off on a drinking spree. Then he gets impossible to be with or to try to have him take any pictures."

Tom asked, "Have you talked to him after he sent you the picture of Jenny?"

"No."

Tom asked, "Would you try to call him to see if would talk with me to see if someone paid him something to let them know when Jenny would be coming out of the hotel?"

"Sure, I'll call him."

Lucy picked up her cell phone and called Steve Black. No answer, Lucy left a message asking Steve to call her."

Lucy said, "I left him a message asking him to call me, but I have no idea how long it maybe before he gets my message."

Tom said, "Thank you for your help and if you hear from Steve please give me a call and see if he will talk with me. Frankly, Lucy, I think Steve may have been paid by someone to let them know when Jenny and I were coming out of the hotel because someone did their best to kill me when I came out of the hotel."

Lucy promised she would call him when she heard from Steve.

CHAPTER FOURTEEN

WHO ARE THESE PEOPLE WHO ARE DOING THEIR BEST TO KILL TOM PARKER?

Tom was still in bed when he heard his cell phone ringing. Tom answered his phone and said, "Tom Parker."

A young woman said, "Tom, it's Lucy Brown, and I've just been contacted by the police and they told me they found Steve Black's body in an alleyway and he had been shot and killed."

"Lucy, I'm so sorry to hear that. I'm afraid they were concerned he might tell me who paid him for letting them know when I was coming out of the Claridge Hotel."

"Tom Parker, you've got to find them and make them pay for killing Steve."

"Lucy, I'll do my best to find them and make them pay for killing Steve and for trying to kill me."

"Good, Tom. If I can do anything to help you just let me know."

"OK, Lucy you can do something to help me find out where Steve's body was found and where he had been last night."

"I'll do my best to get all of the information that I can from the police and check where his body was found. Then I'll check where he had he had been drinking."

"Thanks Lucy. I'll be waiting for your call."

Tom got out of bed and went into the bathroom and was soon in the shower. After finishing his shower, he shaved, tamed his hair the best he could and brushed his teeth. Tom took one more look in the mirror and thought, well, this is the as good as it going to get. I might as well get dressed to be ready to roll as soon as I heard from Lucy.

Jenny had gotten up soon after Tom was up and put on a pot of decaf coffee and went into the other bathroom and was soon in the shower. By the time she had her shower, dried off and applied her make-up and fixed her hair and got dressed, she found Tom had almost emptied the coffee pot.

Jenny said, "Good morning, Tom. I'm glad to see you left me a cup of coffee."

"No problem, my love, I'11 put on another pot of decaf coffee for you."

Tom got up from the table and poured Jenny a cup of coffee and set it down in front of Jenny. Then, he quickly began putting on another pot of decaf coffee.

Next, he leaned down and gave Jenny a good morning kiss. Then said, "I guess you understood what the telephone call from Lucy Brown was all about."

"Yes, I understood that Steve Black's body was found this morning in some alleyway, why is that so important to us."

"My love, it's important to us because he might have been able to tell us who paid him to let them know when we were coming out of the hotel so they could try to kill us or just me."

"OK, that's a good reason to find out who paid him to alert them when we were coming out of the hotel."

"Jenny, it seems like that's about the only lead we may get to try to find out who is working so hard to kill us."

"Tom, I think it more likely that it just you that they want to kill. I doubt they care one way or the other about killing me."

"You may be right."

"I'm pretty sure I right, since you are the CIA's big time-agent that's been after international terrorists for years and you've gotten a lot of them."

"I guess I haven't gotten the ones that are after us right now."

"But you did capture one of them who was trying to kill you and he's in custody of Scotland Yard's right now."

"You know, Jenny, I need to see if I can question him, maybe he might tell us something that could help us and maybe he could get a reduced sentence if he helped us."

"Well, Tom, it's worth a try."

Tom took out his cell phone and placed a call to Captain Hayes and when he answered the call.

Tom said, "Hello, Captain Hayes, this is Tom Parker with the CIA and I would like to know if you could arrange a meeting between the man who was trying to kill me and myself. I would like to see if I could get some information from him on why these people are trying so hard to kill me?"

"Well, I would be happy to do that, but at the moment he is in the hospital after he tried to kill himself."

"How in the hell did he do that?"

When he was given his dinner last night, he took his plastic knife with the serrated blade that they give out to eat with along with a plastic spoon and fork. Anyway, he kept cutting himself in the neck until he caused a massive blood loss."

"He's currently in intensive care at the Queen's Hospital and it's still questionable if he is going to survive. We have our people stationed next to him to be sure he doesn't have another chance of trying to kill himself again."

"I' ll be dammed. I never thought he would try to kill himself and trying to use a little plastic knife to do it. I don't see how he could have ever penetrated the skin to cut his blood vessels with that little plastic knife. I really don't believe it. Plus, I just thought he liked killing other people, not himself."

Captain Hayes responded, "I guess he wasn't happy about you getting away, apparently he had never failed killing people before. We know he's the man who killed at least six people this year in London."

"What makes you think that?"

"We matched his fingerprints with fingerprints that we found at the scene of six unsolved murders in the London this year. So we are pretty happy that he tried to kill you and you caught him for us, thanks."

Tom replied, "I guess you're welcome, but I think you should have a search of his cell. I just can't believe he could do that much damage to his neck with a little plastic knife that caused that much bleeding."

"OK, Tom, I'll have our people recheck that cell to see if he had access to something else that wasn't found there before."

"Captain, if you get word he is going to recover, would you give me a call to see if I might be able to get him to tell me who he was working for?"

"I doubt that he's going to recover and if he does. I double doubt that he would ever tell you anything."

"I'm sure you're right, but I still would like the chance of talking with him."

"OK, Tom Parker, if he recovers. I'll be sure you can talk with him. Like I said before, thank you for getting this guy because you did a great job saving your own life and helping us solve six other murders this year."

"Anytime, just let me know if you need any help solving anymore murders."

"Seriously, Agent Parker, if our man gets so he's able to talk. I'll give you a call to see if you can get him to talk to you.

CHAPTER FIFTEEN

THE PRESIDENT IS CALLING

Almost as soon as Tom was finished talking with Captain Hayes, his cell phone sounded that Tom had an incoming call. Tom answered his phone, "Tom Parker."

Tom heard a voice say, "General Parker, the President wishes to speak with you."

Tom replied, "Yes, ma'am. I'm ready whenever the President is ready."

"One moment, please."

Then Tom heard, "Hi, Tom, how are things going with your investigation?"

"Well, sir, I'm not sure, but since Jenny and I have been in London on this investigation we have had several attempts on our lives."

"I'm so sorry to hear that, Tom, are you both all right?"

"Yes, sir, we are both OK."

"How is your investigation going concerning the Prime Minster and this Russian Businessman?"

"I don't think there is any problem with the Russian Businessman's relationship with the Prime Minster. Sir, I believe it's just two men who met and truly became good friends."

"The one thing we found out is that the Prime Minster is the one paying everything when they are going on these trips. The only thing he's not paying for is the actual tickets to attend the ballets. So it's not a case of a foreign person spending a large amount of money to influence a government official."

"The Prime Minister and Peter Valkovich are just good friends and they like being together; in fact, it looks like Peter is actually going to be going to work for my wife's company."

"How in the hell did that happen, Tom?"

"Sir, after the Chinese completely took over Hong Kong, my wife found that she couldn't continue her business there. So her family and most of her key employees moved to Singapore, but it's much harder for her company to keep doing business in the European market from Singapore than it was from Hong Kong."

"We told everyone that was the reason we were in London, so Jenny could establish a regional office and warehouse in London to work the European market. We have been using that as a way to investigate the association between the Prime Minster and Peter Valkovich."

"That gave us a way to meet with the Prime Minster, which led to us having a meeting with Peter Valkovich. After a couple meetings with him, Peter contacted a real estate agent for Jenny and she was very impressed with the new port location that's in north east of London and she actually decided to set up a new facility there for her company to serve the European Market."

"After that, Peter Valkovich contacted Jenny and asked her for the job as the Director of European Operations for her European Company. He explained that since the war that was started by Russia against Ukraine, he had lost so much of his business that he needed a job."

"Tom, how does any of this explain the number of times you have had people trying to kill you?"

"Mr. President, I don't have any idea, except one of the people told me on the phone they didn't like me looking around in Europe and they had to kill me."

Then the President asked, "Do you have any idea what they think you are looking around Europe for?"

"No, sir, I don't have a clue."

"Tom, I think maybe you should keep looking around in Europe to see if you can come up with what these people are so concerned about what you might find."

"All right, sir, Jenny and I will keep, as you said, looking around in Europe to see if we can find out what these folks are so worried about us finding."

"One last thing, General Parker, be sure you keep yourself and your wife safe and alive, that's an order, General Parker."

"Yes, sir."

The President hung up his phone.

"Well, Jenny, the President told me that my job was to keep us both safe and alive, and that it was an order."

"All right, General, you damn well better carry out the President's order, General Parker."

"Yes ma'am, I'll do my best to carry out the President's order."

"Well, I truly hope you do it."

Tom just took Jenny into his arms and gave her one of the biggest kisses she had ever had in her whole life."

When Tom released her and took his arms from around her waist she said, "Well, that was some kiss. From now on, if I feel like I'm not getting enough kisses, I'm just going to call the President and ask him to give you an order to be sure to keep me alive."

"My love, I'm sure the President would drop everything and give me a call if you called him to let him know that you needed another kiss like that one."

"Damn right he would."

"You are probably right. He would be afraid you might give his opponent a big donation."

"Well, I might, but it would only be someone that I thought would be a better president than he is."

Tom was saved by his phone when it told him he had a call. Tom took up his phone and said, "Tom Parker."

"Tom, this is Captain Hayes and you're right. After my people searched the cell again they found a six inch switch blade knife tucked into one of the pillows in his cell with his blood on it."

"Thank you Captain Hayes, I didn't think he could do that kind of damage to his throat with a little plastic knife."

"No, Tom, he didn't. The question is now, how did he get a knife like that in his cell?"

"So, I guess you are going to be busy trying to find out how he managed to get a knife like that."

"Yes, I'm afraid we will be very busy trying to find out just how that could happen. I'll talk with you later."

Tom turned off his phone and heard Jenny's cell phone ringing.

Jenny answered her cell phone and he heard Jenny say, "Hello, whose calling?"

Jenny heard, "Hello, Jenny Parker, this is Suri Pearson and I wanted to invite you to have lunch with me tomorrow if you are available."

Jenny replied, "Suri, it would be my pleasure."

"Great, then I will pick you up at your hotel at eleven tomorrow morning and we will be going to our country club for lunch. Then we can talk about our husbands and all of their faults."

Then Jenny could hear Suri laughing at what she had just said.

Jenny said, "Well, that should be fun, but it might have to be a very long lunch for me to list all of my husband's faults."

Jenny could hear Suri laughing even more.

Jenny then said, "Sometimes I can't remember why I love him so much."

Suri added, "Yes, sometimes, that's a problemwith my husband too."

Jenny replied, "OK, Suri, I'm looking forward to seeing you tomorrow at eleven. Goodbye, Suri."

"Great, I'll see you at eleven, Jenny."

CHAPTER SIXTEEN

THE PLOT THICKENS

The next morning Jenny told Tom they needed to get over to the Claridge Hotel by ten o'clock to be sure they were in their suite before Suri came there to pick her up for lunch at her country club.

Tom said, "I'm ready to go anytime you are. Benny's here with the limo, so we can leave whenever you're ready."

A little after nine, Jenny told Tom she was ready to go. They were soon in the limo and they arrived at the Claridge Hotel in record time. They were there only a few minutes after ten.

Jenny's phone rang about fifteen minutes before eleven. It was Suri telling Jenny they were just arriving at the hotel. Jenny said she would come right down and meet her.

Jenny gave Tom a kiss and said, "I have no idea how long this lunch is going to last, so I'll see you when I get back."

When Jenny arrived in the lobby, she saw Suri waiting near the front door of the hotel.

Jenny thought Suri was a very beautiful woman and knew she must have really stood out when she was dressed in her ballerina outfits.

Suri greeted Jenny warmly and the two of them went out to the driveway in front of the hotel. There, Suri's driver, Charles, was waiting to open the doors of the limo for Suri and Jenny. Suri and Jenny were soon in the backseat of the limo and Charles closed the doors was soon in the driver's seat and starting the car.

Charles pulled the limo out of the hotel's driveway and a security car pulled ahead of him and a second security car got in back of the limo.

Jenny said, "Suri, I see you have security officers in cars before your limo and another one following behind us."

Suri replied, "That's something that goes on anytime I am out of 10 Downing Street. It's just to protect me because I'm the wife of the Prime Minster. Sometimes, I think it was nicer when I was just a British citizen, not the wife of the Prime Minister. But I know it's how things are, and I think Blake is doing a great job as Prime Minster."

Jenny replied, "Yes, I understand that's the way it has to be. Who knows what some of these crazy terrorists or criminals might do."

About that time Jenny saw a large truck pull in front of the security car following Suri's limo. Then Jenny heard shots being fired from the back of the large truck.

Then she saw that the security car that had been following behind the limo collided into a car parked on the street.

Then the large truck was making its way pass the limo and Jenny told Suri to get down on the floor of the limo and she did the same.

The next thing the large truck did was to pull ahead of the limo and run into the security car in front of the limo and pushed it into a car parked on the street.

When that happened, Charles sped around the large truck and then a car pulled up behind the limo and ran into the back bumper of the limo and the car kept pushing the limo until it hit a car coming on the other side of the traffic lane. The limo and the car it hit suddenly stopped.

During all of this, Suri and Jenny had stayed on the floor of the limo. Suddenly, the two back doors were opened and two very large men grabbed hold of Jenny and Suri and pulled them out of the limo and roughly put them on the floor in the back of a panel truck, then closed and locked the door.

Then the panel truck began speeding away from the wrecked vehicles, and Jenny and Suri where sliding from one side of the truck to the other side.

Finally, Jenny grabbed hold of a handle with her right hand on the right side of the panel truck and grabbed Suri's right hand with her left hand and they stopped sliding. It also helped because the panel truck was now going down the road in a straight line.

Jenny looked to the front of the panel truck and could see two men. One was driving the panel truck and the other man seemed to be giving directions to the driver.

Jenny and Suri tried to think of what just had happened to them and why these men had taken them.

The two men in the front of the panel truck had no conversation except the man on the left of the driver kept give the driver directions, otherwise, they said nothing.

The two women continued to lie on the floor of the panel truck and Jenny kept trying to see her watch and finally she saw it was now almost twelve thirty. So they had been traveling almost an hour and half. The panel truck had no windows on the side of the truck and only a couple of small windows in the back doors of the panel truck, and lying on the floor they couldn't see out the windshield or much out of the two side windows in the front of the truck.

Jenny couldn't tell if they were still in the city or out in the country.

After they traveled on for another thirty minutes, the man who wasn't driving asked, "Are you ladies all right laying on that plywood floor?"

Jenny replied, "Well, it's not the best ride I've ever had, and if the truth be known, it's the worst ride I've ever taken."

Then the man asked, "How about you, pretty girl?"

"Well, I like my rides sitting in a nice limo and the driver taking me where I want to go."

Then the man said, "Who knows, you may like where we are taking you."

Suri replied, "I doubt it and I don't think you are going to like the ride you are going to get when my husband's people catch you."

The man said, "I wouldn't be too sure about that, Mrs. Pearson, first they have to catch us."

The driver told the man who had been doing all of the talking, "You better shut up before the boss finds out about you saying anything to Mrs. Pearson. He won't like it and he's killed more people for a lot less than what you're doing. He told us to do our job and keep our mouths shut."

Then the man who had been talking before said, "How about you, Chinese lady, will your husband be happy you're not going to be home tonight to fix his dinner?"

Jenny replied, "If I were you, I wouldn't be worried about what your boss might do to you because my husband will likely make you wish you had never been born."

The mouthy man said, "Your man is tough, is he? Well, he's never been up against me."

Jenny said, "Tough are you? I've see him take on ten like you all at the same time and finish them all off."

Then the driver said, "Jackson, shut up before I kill you myself."

"You should just try."

About that time the driver pulled off the highway and began driving up a country road, and after driving about another half mile or so, he pulled up in front of a small farm house.

The driver told the other man "Let's get the ladies into the house. I'm sure they will be more comfortable then laying on the floor of this dumb panel truck.

Jenny said as she got out of the truck, "Well, it's not best place I've ever laid down."

The driver said, "I am really sorry about that, Mrs. Pearson, but it was the best we could do for the job we had."

The driver asked, "Chinese lady, what do you do for Mrs. Pearson and what's your name?"

"My name Jenny and I do whatever Mrs. Pearson asks me do."

"It figures, you could never get an English woman to work for her to do all the things you have to do."

"No, Mrs. Pearson nice me, treat me well."

The man then said, "I'm sorry you got caught up with Mrs. Pearson when we took her, we didn't need anybody else but her. Our boss wanted her so he could get one of our people out of jail."

Suri understood what Jenny was doing with the way she was talking.

CHAPTER SEVENTEEN

THEY DON'T KNOW WHAT THEY'VE GOTTEN THEMSELVES INTO

The television was on in the lobby of the Claridge Hotel as Tom was making his way for lunch. Then he heard the TV reporter say "It's unbelievable that the wife of Prime Minister Pearson has been kidnapped from her limo and her two security cars were wrecked in central London this morning. We now take you to our reporter who is on site with more information on this story.

Tom sat down and listened to the reporter who said, "The police have confirmed that Mrs. Suri Pearson and another lady traveling with her were kidnapped out of her limo around eleven o'clock this morning in central London. The kidnappers caused her two security cars to be wrecked and then her limo. Then she and another lady were taken out of the limo and placed in a small panel truck that soon got away from the scene. More news on this story when we have more information!"

Tom called Captain Hayes at police headquarters. His called went through very quickly and Tom heard, "This is Captain Hayes, how can I help you?"

Tom said, "It's Tom Parker and I just heard that Mrs. Pearson has been kidnapped and my wife is with her."

"My God, man, how in the hell was she with her?"

"Mrs. Pearson invited her to lunch at her country club."

"Damn, do you think they have any idea who they have along with Mrs. Pearson?"

"Well, I hope they don't. I don't need any more problems than what I have with people trying to kill us every time we turn around."

"Tom, do you think they may have been after her instead of Mrs. Pearson?"

"I don't have any idea. I just have to hope they don't know who she is."

"Tom, you keep praying they don't"

"There's no worry about that. I'm sending up prayers even as we're talking."

"Tom, there is one thing you should know. We now have cameras on almost every block in the City of London and our people are going over them as we speak to see if we can find that panel truck that the women are reported to be in. That way we may be able to find out where that vehicle went."

"Captain Hayes, please keep me informed and if I get any information, I'll give you a call."

When Tom got off the phone, he remembered something that had happened the last time they were in Washington D.C. The CIA had implanted a location chip into Jenny's left shoulder like the one they did for Tom years before.

Tom quickly called CIA Headquarters in the USA and asked to speak with Ron Parson, the Director of the CIA.

Less than two minutes later, Tom heard Ron answer the phone and saying, "Well, General Tom Parker, are you still willing to talk with me? I thought you only worked for the President now, even though you and your wife are on my payroll."

Tom replied, "First, I want to congratulate you for finally getting to be the Director of the CIA, it's certainly about time. You've been running the company a long time before you actually got the job and you certainly deserve to have it."

"Next, I want to ask you to quickly have your people run satellite tracking and find out where Jenny is. She and the wife of the British Prime Minster have been kidnapped in central London today."

"Hang on, Tom. I'll get the information on where Jenny is located."

Ron put Tom on hold and called the people in the tracking department and told them he wanted the location of where CIA Agent Jenny Parker was located. He added please find that as quickly as you can and call me right back with the information because she's been kidnapped.

Then Ron switched back over to Tom and said, "Tom, I'm so sorry to hear about Jenny being taken, but how in the heck did that happen?"

"Ron, Jenny was going to a lunch with the Prime Minister's wife, Suri Pearson, and they were both kidnapped in central London. We know they were taken somewhere outside of London and I'm pretty worried they may decide that she is just a nobody, so they might decide to just get rid of her."

"Tom, I think if they took any kind of a look at her, they would quickly decide she was somebody."

Ron then saw he had a call from the folks in the tracking center and told Tom to hold on. Ron answered the call and they gave him the co-ordinates of Jenny's current location. Ron thanked them and said he would pass the information on to Tom Parker and he would be keeping in touch with them and for them to keep tracking Jenny Parker's location.

If there is any change in her position, let Tom know at once. Ron gave Tom, Jenny's current co-ordinates and asked him if he needed anything else at this time.

Tom told him, "No. I think with help from British Scotland Yard, we should be OK." Tom thanked Ron for his and the tracking people's help.

Tom then called Captain Hayes at Scotland Yard and when the Captain answered the phone. Tom said, "I have the co-ordinates of where my wife and Suri Pearson are currently being held."

Captain Hayes said, "OK, but how do you know where she is? We got every police officer in the UK searching for Suri Pearson."

"Because they took my wife with her and my wife is a CIA Agent with a tracking chip under her skin. I called CIA Headquarters and they gave me the information on where my wife is located."

"OK, that's great Agent Parker, but you'll have to get some of your people who know how to use those co-ordinates things to help us find where your wife is and, hopefully, that where Mrs. Pearson is, she's with her."

Tom called Robert Clark and told him he needed him to help recover Jenny and Mrs. Pearson, so bring a map so you can show the police how the co-ordinates work and you can tell Captain Hayes where the women are being held. The three of them soon met at Scotland Yard and Robert showed Captain Hayes the location where the women were being held, using the map's co-ordinates to pin point the exact location of where Jenny was being held.

Tom called CIA Headquarters and got the update from the tracking center and they confirmed Jenny was still at the same location.

Captain Hayes soon had a small army of police officers armed with automatic weapons and they were ready to handle the people holding Jenny and Suri Pearson. As soon as they were assembled, Captain Hayes had them load up in armored vehicles.

Captain Hayes had Tom and Robert seated next to the driver of the lead vehicle and they were soon on their way traveling south of London and the driver kept asking Robert if he thought the women were still in the same location.

He assured him the satellites confirmed that Jenny was still at the same co-ordinates as she had been.

Almost an hour later they were approaching a small road off to the right, where the coordinates told them was where Jenny was.

Captain Hayes asked, "Tom, since you are an Army man and we are in an area out in the countryside. How do you think we should proceed to where Jenny and Mrs. Pearson are been held?

Tom told him the best thing I think we should do is to take your police officers out of their vehicles and divide them into two platoons, have one platoon go on the left side in the woods of the little road that's leading into this property and the second platoon go up the right side of the road in the woods. Each of these platoons should have the officers spread out at least two to three feet apart, so they can make sure no one can slip out between them trying to escape out of the property. We want to catch or kill every one of them.

Tom said, "Leave the drivers with their vehicles and have them block the exit with their vehicles and be prepared to stop anyone from trying to leave the property. If they try to leave, shoot them."

Captain Hayes had already checked up on Tom Parker and knew his army background and said, "You heard the General, do as he said.

Divide up into two platoons. One platoon, go up the right side of the road and the second platoon go up the left side."

"Then you drivers get your vehicles and park them so they are completely blocking the entrance of the road and if any of them try to leave the property, shoot them."

The officers divided up. One platoon went to the right side of the road and a second platoon went to the left side of the road.

Then Tom said, "Captain Hayes, I think you better stay with the vehicles so you can be ready in case we need more help getting these people. You and your people can capture or kill any of them that get past us."

"OK, General Parker. I'll stay here with the men and their vehicles."

Tom then started right up the middle of the little road leading up to whatever was ahead. He didn't know what was ahead of him but he knew Jenny was up there waiting for him. What he did know for sure was that the satellites told him his love was somewhere ahead of him.

Step by step, he continued up that little road and he could see the well-armed police officers moving along on both sides of him as he told them to do.

The little road certainly wasn't a straight road leading up to the unknown. It twisted and turned, it seemed like every few steps.

The trees and the brush were pretty thick and he could tell his police officers were having a pretty hard time making the climb. As bad as his old legs were, it was pretty hard for him to do it and he was on the center of the little road.

He continued walking for what seemed like a long time before got a glance of the little house in front of him. The house looked like it was perfect little hideaway, all right.

Before he got all of the way up to the house he got off of the little road on the right side and made his way over to where one of the police officer's was and that he was carrying a bullhorn.

Tom told the officer to stop and mot move out into the opening where the house is.

Tom signaled to the officers on each side of the road to spread out and circle around the house and stay hidden in the woods.

Now, Tom could see the panel truck that looked like what he had been told it looked like by the people who saw the women being put into the back of it.

When the officers had completely surrounded the house, Tom asked the officer that had been carrying the bullhorn to give the microphone to him. At this time, it was as quiet as it could be with only a few birds chirruping in the woods close to the house.

Then Tom put the mike close to his lips and announced, "The house is completely surrounded with police officers. Come out of the house with your hands in the air and send the two women you are holding out in front of you."

He didn't hear any reply or see anyone coming out of the house.

Inside the house, the men were shocked to hear an American voice over a loud speaker.

Then one of the men said, "How can this be happening? No one could have found us this quick. We did just like we were told to do."

Jenny now said in her regular voice, "I can tell you one thing. That voice you heard is my husband and he's not going to let any of you leave alive if you don't do as he says.

So you better give up and walk out that door. It's your only chance to keep living."

The man said, "Shut up, lady, or I'm going to kill you."

"OK, go ahead, but you can plan on being dead along with me. My husband will never let you live if you touch me."

The man said, "Are you crazy, lady? The police wouldn't let him kill me."

"You don't know anyone like him and you never will."

The man just looked at Jenny with a strange look in his eyes. He didn't know what to think. Then he said, "I think I just got to kill you, lady, right now."

Jenny replied, "Go ahead and when my husband gets here and sees my dead body you are going to die, but before you do you'll be begging for him to finish killing you due to all the pain you'll be in."

While this was going on, Suri Pearson just stood back as far as she could away from Jenny and just kept crying.

Finally the driver said, "Bud, you crazy man, open that damn door and let the women go outside and throw your gun away and give up and let's keep living."

Just then Tom said, using the bullhorn, "OK, you people have had your chance and now I'm coming in to get you."

The driver opened the door and told Jenny and Suri to quickly go outside before that crazy man kills all of us.

Tom had already started out of the woods and was moving quickly toward the house's door, but when he saw the door swing open, he hit the ground with his automatic aimed at the door to shoot whoever came out the door, but then he saw Jenny walking out of the door and Suri had her hand on Jenny's arm and was following right behind her.

Now the police officers all begin moving quickly out of the woods and were soon inside the house and bringing the two men outside in handcuffs.

One of the officers radioed Captain Hayes and soon after that the police vehicles were pulling up to the house.

Before the two men were put into police vehicles the one man said to Jenny who was holding on to Tom, "So, this is the man who was going to make me beg him to kill me so I wouldn't have any more pain, is that right, lady? He don't look so tough to me, lady."

Tom replied, "Looking and talking tough, doesn't make you tough, action does."

Just then the man broke free from the officers that were holding on to him and he made a run at Tom.

Tom saw him coming and moved away from Jenny, and when the man got close to Tom, Tom took his right hand and hit the man in the throat and down he went. Then, Tom gave the man a kick in the side with his left foot, then reached down and picked the man up and gave him one more hit in his nose, breaking his nose and blood was pouring out of it, and down the man went again.

Then the two officers picked the man up and put him in the police vehicle.

By this time, Blake Pearson arrived in his limo, along with his two security vehicles, and Suri came running to him as he was getting out of his car. Blake reached out and took Suri into arms and held her as close to his body as possible.

After several minutes passed, Prime Minster Pearson thanked Captain Hayes and his men for doing a wonderful job of rescuing his wife.

However, Captain Hayes said, "Sir, all the thanks have to go to General Parker and his wife for their rescue. They were found so quickly because Mrs. Parker is a CIA Agent and has a device under her skin that the CIA can use their satellites to track her any place on earth."

Then Blake turned to Tom and said, "Thank you and your wife for saving Suri. It's greatly appreciated. I'll have to have a talk with your President to see if I can get one of those devices put under Suri's skin so I can keep track of her."

Suri said, "Jenny, thank you so much for helping me stay together for all we went through, I love you. As soon as I am back to being myself, I'll call you and have you and Tom for the weekend."

Jenny replied, "Suri, you were very brave going through all of this. I'll have a special place in my heart for you. I love you, too."

CHAPTER EIGHTEEN

SO NOW WHAT DO WE DO?

Tom asked Captain Hayes if he could interrogate the prisoners and was told he could. However, he would have to allow a police officer to be present when he did.

Tom said, "I think my best chance of getting any information would be to talk with the fellow that didn't take after me when they were arrested."

Captain Hayes replied, "That sounds like the best choice to me. I'll have him taken to a holding room for us to talk to him."

A few minutes passed and Captain Hayes got a call telling him that the prisoner was in Holding Room One.

Captain Hayes and Tom made their way to Holding Room One and on their arrival, Captain Hayes said, "Tom, since it was your wife being held, I think you should be the one asking the questions."

"All right, I just have a few questions for this man. First question I have for you should be pretty easy, "What is your full name?"

The prisoner replied, "Charles Wilson Taylor, but everybody just calls me Charlie."

"OK, Charlie, I'll do that. How long have you working with these people?"

"A couple of years."

"So what do you do for these people?"

"I drive."

"Do you always drive around in that panel truck?"

"No, I never drove it before the job we had today."

"Where did you get the truck?"

"Donald found it parked in a parking lot by a small grocery store."

"In other words, you just stole the truck for this job."

"I guess so; Donald said we'11 just leave our car outside the parking lot, 'cause we were going to come back and get it later."

"Have you ever been in jail or prison before?"

"No, sir, all I ever did was drive vehicles for people."

"Did you work for a lot of people?"

"Yes, the company I work for, they had lots of companies I drive for. I drove for different people in this company that I'm driving for all the time now."

"Tell me about these people what are their names?"

"I don't know exactly what their names were. They were just called by their jobs."

"Can you tell me some of those names?"

"Sure, one of the names was a guy called, 'The Enforcer', another one was called, 'The Negotiator ' then one was called, 'Fixer,''and the last one was called, 'The Terminator' and they all worked for the 'Big Guy'." "You mean you actually don't know any of these people's names?"

"No just their job's names."

"Well, how about the Big Guy, you never heard his name either?"

"Nope, I never even drove him anyplace. In fact I never saw the guy."

"So you never saw this guy at all?"

"No, I never saw him or drove him anywhere."

"You mean, you worked for this gang for over two years and you never saw the big boss or knew what any of any these guys' actual names were?"

"That's right. I guess they didn't want me to know who they were."

"How did you get paid?"

"I got paid every Friday."

"Who paid you?"

"The Negotiator."

"How did he pay you?"

"In cash."

"How much did you get paid every week?"

"I got paid four hundred pounds a week."

"Isn't that a pretty good salary every week for driving people around?"

"Well, it's not wonderful, but it's better than most of the other drivers got paid."

"Did you get to keep all of that money every week?"

"No, I had to give the company that I work for ten percent of my pay."

"Charlie, what do you think these people did that you were driving them around for?"

"I didn't have any idea. I thought they had some kind of finance business, because it seemed like when I drove the Negotiator around every Friday, he was always picking up money at every stop we made. We did the same route every week."

"So what did you think about stealing the panel truck?"

"I didn't know what to think. I've never been involved in anything like that before. I had no idea what was going on but when Jackson took those two ladies out of that limousine I was just scared."

Tom said, "Charlie, are you as dumb as you sound like you are?"

"Probably, I kind of figured out the people who I'd been working for were dealing drugs about a month ago, but I never said anything to anybody about it. Because I thought if they knew that I thought they were dealing drugs, they would have probably killed me and I have to help my Mommy to have enough money to buy food and pay our rent. My Mommy told me so."

Tom replied, "You're probably right, Charlie, they might have killed you to keep you from talking to the police."

"But when they kidnapped those ladies, it was too much for me. I'm so glad you got them free, are they both all right?"

"They're OK, they are just trying to get to feeling better and stop worrying about what was going to happen to them next."

"I'm really sorry about those nice ladies. I really thought they were going to get killed."

"Charlie, do you want to help us get those bad people? Because if you do, can you take us where the Negotiator lives?"

"No, I only know where I picked him up from."

"Would you take us to where you picked him up right now?" "I can't, because I'm in jail."

"Well, Charlie, what if I get you out of jail, could you take Captain Hayes and me there?"

"Sure I could, but I don't have a car."

"It's OK. Captain Hayes can get a car for you to drive, can't you, Captain?"

"Sure, I've got a car you can drive, Charlie."

"OK, then I can take you both. But, do I have to wear this funny looking uniform when I'm driving?"

Captain Hayes replied, "No, Charlie I can let you wear your own uniform."

"OK, let me change my clothes and I'll take you where I pick up the Negotiator."

Captain Hayes told the officer standing outside the holding cell to have someone bring this prisoner his street clothes."

Only a few minutes passed and an officer brought Charlie his clothes and shoes and all of the items he had in his pockets when he was arrested. Charlie soon dressed and Captain Hayes, Tom and Charlie made their way out of the police station into a parking garage and to the Captain's car.

Charlie got into the car behind the wheel and the Captain sat down in the front seat next to Charlie. Then the Captain gave Charlie the keys to the car.

Tom was seated directly behind Charlie in case Charlie was not as dumb as he seemed to be.

Charlie asked, "OK, Captain, is it all right to start the car and go now?"

The Captain replied, "OK, Charlie, please take us to where you picked up the Negotiator every Friday."

Charlie started the car and carefully backed out of the parking space and he was soon on his way to where he picked up the Negotiator every Friday.

Charlie drove for about thirty-five minutes and asked the Captain if he wanted him to park in front of the building and the Captain replied, "No Charlie, I just want you drive by very slowly. So I can get the address and then I want you to drive the route you drove every Friday going to each stopping place that you did when you went on your Friday route."

Charlie said, "OK, Captain. I can do that since we made the same stops every week I can remember every one of them."

"That's good, Charlie; you may be getting yourself a "Get out of jail free card" if you can help us catch all of the people in that gang that's dealing drugs."

"That would make my poor Mommy very happy, because she never wanted me to ever get into any kind of trouble."

They spent almost eight hours driving Charlie's Friday's stops. The Captain recorded each address on the stops that Charlie's made when he had been driving the Negotiator on his Friday route.

When they returned to the police station, the Captain said, "Charlie, you did a great service to the police department because using this information, we may be able to stop a lot of drugs being sold on the streets here in London. Plus, it will let us put a lot of those people in prison for selling those drugs."

"Charlie, the bad news is we need to put you into protective custody, but I can tell you that we will also get your mother and have the two of you in a place that will keep both of you safe until we get all of these people in prison."

"But, Captain, I thought you said I was going to get a "Get out of jail free card. I didn't think you were going to keep me in jail and put my Mommy in jail with me."

"Charlie, you and your mother are not going to be in jail. You'll have a nice place to live and have people looking after you and bring you plenty of food and almost anything either one of you want. Do you have anybody else in your family?"

"No, but my Mommy has lots of friends."

"It will be OK; we will just tell them you are both gone on a long holiday trip."

"Oh, Captain, I hope my Mommy won't be too unhappy by not having her friends."

"Oh, she can be making new friends with the people looking after both of you."

They didn't return to the police station. Instead, they drove directly to Mommy's house and the Captain said, "Charlie, let me go in to talk with your mother by myself first, OK."

"OK, if you think that's best."

"I do."

The Captain walked to the door and knocked on the door and when Charlie's mother opened the door and saw a policeman there she asked,"Is Charlie all right?"

The Captain said, "Yes, he's is OK, he just got caught up in a police matter."

"Is he in jail?"

"No, he's in my police car and he is OK and he is now in protective custody."

"What does that mean officer?"

"It means we are going to keep him safe from some of the people he has been driving for.

In fact, we want you to come and go with him so these people won't try to harm you."

"Why would they try to harm me?"

"Because they would do it to keep your son from testifying against them. He didn't know it, but these are really bad people, and if they could find him, they would kill him and kill you, too."

"OK, officer. I'll go with you but do I have time to pack some clothes for us?"

"Yes, you do, but I'll have you son come help you get his things together. OK?"

Captain Hayes went back to his car and told Charlie he could get out of the car and help his mother pack his clothes and anything else he would need to go on a long trip."

Charlie got out of the car and went into the house and Captain Hayes took a seat under the wheel and told Tom to get in the front seat.

Next, the Captain radioed headquarters and asked them to send two squad cars ASAP to the address he was giving them, but no sirens.

A few minutes later, two more police cars pulled up behind the Captain's vehicle. He got out of his car and told the officers in the cars to just wait in their cars and then follow him while he took a couple of witnesses to a safe house.

Then, the Captain went back into the house and found Charlie and his mother were just finishing packing and were ready to go out to his car.

Mommy locked the house and Charlie carried out two very old suitcases to the car.

They were soon inside the car with their suitcases now in the boot of the car.

Thirty minutes later, the car pulled into a driveway and a lady opened the front door of the house and let Charlie and Mommy into the house. Then the lady showed them two bedrooms, each bedroom had its own bathroom.

Captain Hayes told Charlie and his Mommy, "This lady is your housekeeper and your cook. Her name is Ruth and she will be looking after you during your stay."

If you need something, you just tell Ruth and she will get it for you. We do have other people who will be looking after the exterior of the house and neither one of you are allowed to go outside of the house. Enjoy your stay and Ruth and her helpers will do a great job looking after you."

"If for any reason Ruth has to leave anytime during your stay. Someone else will be in the house looking after both of you."

Then the Captain and Tom told Charlie and his Mommy good bye and to enjoy their stay.

CHAPTER NINETEEN

NOW WE KNOW WE WERE DEALING WITH DRUG DEALERS

Tom told Captain Hayes, We know now we are dealing with drug dealers and not with international terrorists, but the big question is, are these the people who have been trying to kill me and Jenny ever since we arrived in London?

Captain Hayes asked, "What do you think, Tom ? You're the expert dealing with terrorists?"

"Plus, I need to turn this case over to our drug investigation team. I certainly want to know if they had any idea that these people were such big time operators in the drug business in the UK."

Tom replied, "Well, if they didn't, they should have known about them."

"That's what I'm thinking, Tom, how could any gang dealing with that many different sales points not be known by somebody in the drug enforcement division?"

Tom said, "Perhaps, maybe instead of telling them about the problem, you need to have some investigation of the folks who are running that department or the people who cover those parts of the city."

"Tom, that's the problem. Because the route that Charlie took us on pretty well covers the whole of London. Meaning, our drug enforcement people have been missing one of the major players in the drug business in the city."

"Well, Captain, right now, you are the only person in the Police Department that has any knowledge of how wide-spread these drug dealer's operations are, wouldn't you say?"

"You're right, Tom, and the people we arrested are charged with kidnapping two women, not for dealing drugs."

"So, they may not have any idea that we have this much information on their drug dealing. Plus, the people we arrested have no idea what Charlie may have told us and the story they are going to hear is that Charlie has been sent to a mental institution, since, he's not mentally competent to stand trial for kidnapping."

"Captain, I think that's the best idea. You probably need to have your best detectives that are not involved in drug enforcement investigate your drug detectives to see what they come up with."

"One thing, Captain, I don't think these are the people who have been trying to kill Jenny and myself ever since we arrived in London. I think Jenny just got caught up in the kidnapper's web when they took Mrs. Person. They certainly didn't care anything about Jenny because they thought she was just a servant working for Mrs. Pearson."

"You're lucky, Tom. They had no idea they were holding one of the richest woman in the world."

"Well, we were lucky that we found both Mrs. Pearson and my Jenny and neither of them had been harmed and we found them very quickly."

The Captain replied, "Well, the only reason they were found so quickly was because Jenny had that tracking device in her shoulder. Otherwise, we might not have ever found them or at least not until after the Prime Minster paid a huge sum of money to get his wife back."

Tom said, "Then, the odds of getting them back alive would have been probably next to zero. What we would have probably gotten back was Suri and Jenny's dead bodies after the money was paid."

The Captain said, "I'm very sorry to say it, Tom, but I'm afraid you would be right about that."

"Well, Captain Hayes, I certainly appreciate you and your men helping me get Jenny back safe. I love that woman so much I can't think of living without her."

"Yes, I understand that. I lost my wife a few years ago after loving her for over forty-five years and no one can ever take her place. The people I work with have no idea how tough life is after that kind of a loss."

"No, I'm sure they don't and, again, I thank you and your men for helping freeing the women and capturing the men who took them. I think you've got a lot of work ahead of you, checking on your drug enforcement officers and getting the rest of that drug cartel. Good luck, Captain Hayes."

CHAPTER TWENTY

JENNY IS SAFE BUT HOW ARE THEY EVER GOING TO FIND THE PEOPLE WHO KEEPS TRYING TO KILL THEM

Tom said, "Jenny, I'm certainly glad you agreed to have that tracking device put in your shoulder when you did. I'm pretty sure it saved both yours and Mrs. Pearson's lives."

"You know I only did it because I knew you would have kept after me to do it. So I agreed to have it put in my shoulder and that saved me from having to listen to you every day until I did it."

"See, my love, every once in a while, I have a good idea."

Jenny replied, "Just shut up and hold me in those long arms and keep me safe and make love with me."

"Yes, my love. Your wish is my command."

With that, Tom took her gently in his arms and then they found their way onto their big bed.

Sometime later, Tom said, "My love, we need to find out who else works in Blake Pearson's office that knows where he's going all the time, someone besides his brother Hanson."

"I really thought Hanson was probably the one that was behind the problems we had with people trying to kill us since we arrived in London, but now I don't think he is. I think he is a real brother to Blake and I think he would do everything he could to keep him alive and certainly not try to kill him."

"The other thing that comes to my mind is that maybe someone in the CIA office here in London is playing on the wrong side, but even they don't know everything we are doing all the time."

Jenny said, "You know, Tom, it all seems so hard to believe that any of these people would want to kill you and I don't think they have any thought about killing me, it's only you they want. Oh, they would be willing to kill me, but only because I was with you."

"Jenny, I think you're right about that. So, I think what you should do is go home to LA to be sure you are around to raise Tommy. I don't want you to get killed, just because you're here with me. It will be much safer for you to go back home."

"Tom Parker, you're not sending me home so that I'm safe. I belong here with you and it's your job to see that both of Tommy's parents come back home to him."

"You heard that all right didn't you, Tom Parker? Your job is to take care of you and me."

"Jenny Parker, you're a stubborn woman and you're not going to do what you should do, are you?"

"No, I'm not going home! If you're going to die you're taking me with you. So, do your job and keep both of us alive."

Just at that moment Tom's telephone signaled he had a call.

Tom hesitated before answering the call and Jenny said, "Tom Parker, answer that call."

Tom finally answered, "Tom Parker."

A voice said, "Tom Parker, you don't know me, but I know you. You killed my brother, do you remember him, Dr. Al-Sadr?"

"Well, I'm Uranus Al-Sadr and my people have been trying to kill you and your wife, but so far they've missed, but I won't. So, have a nice day. 'cause your days are numbered."

Then the phone went dead.

Tom turned to Jenny and said, "You are never going to believe this call. It came from a man who said his name was Uranus Al-Sadr and he said he was going to kill me because I killed his brother Dr. Al-Sadr."

"Did you kill his brother?"

"Yes, but he was trying to kill me at that time, as you may remember."

Tom's phone rang again.

Tom looked at Jenny and said, "Maybe it's Uranus Al-Sadr telling me he changed his mind about killing me."

Tom answered his phone, "Tom Parker."

Captain Hayes said, "Tom, I have an idea how we might be able to catch the people who have been trying to kill you."

"That would be really good, since I just had a call from a man who said he's had people trying to kill me, but now he said he would be doing it himself, at least that's what I think he said."

"Why is he trying to kill you?"

"He said some years ago I killed his brother. He had been trying to kill a lot of people in America."

"Do you know what this man's name is, Tom?"

"Yes, he told me his name. It's Uranus Al-Sadr."

"Tom, I've heard of this man's name before. Let me think. I know, I've got it, he some kind of "Good Samaritan.""

"He's always in the newspapers for paying for medical treatments for kids and poor adults when they have no way to pay for some very high cost medical treatments. Many of them have to go to some other country to get these treatments and he pays for all their costs."

"Well, Captain, that's certainly doesn't sound like the man that called me."

"Maybe, somebody else is using his name. His name is in the newspapers and on the TV news all the time."

"Well, I guess that's possible, but I have to doubt it, since he knew that I killed his brother."

Captain Hayes said, "Let me see if I can set up a meeting with Uranus Al-Sadr to discuss if he could help one of my officer's sons who needs to have some treatments in Switzerland. If he doesn't get the treatments soon, they are afraid he going to die."

"OK, Captain, see what you can do."

"All right, Tom. I'll see if I can set up a meeting with him."

An hour later, Captain Hayes called Tom and told him that he had a meeting set up at two o'clock this afternoon with Uranus Al-Sadr to discuss getting him to help pay for the officer's son medical treatments."

Tom told the Captain he would be there at one thirty. Tom and Jenny arrived at the Captain's office at one thirty, as Tom had told him.

Promptly at two o'clock, Uranus Al-Sadr arrived for the meeting with the Captain to discuss providing the funds for the police officer's son.

When Uranus arrived, the Captain introduced him to Tom and Jenny Parker and told Uranus that he had told Tom and Jenny about the officer's son and they offered to help with the funds as well.

Uranus shook hands with Tom and bowed to Jenny and said, "I heard that Jenny Parker was in London working on establishing a branch of her company in London. I think you will be very happy how well your products will be selling in the European Market. This should make your company even bigger than it already is."

Jenny replied, "I'm surprised that you had heard about me being in London."

"London is a pretty big city. However, news about someone who's so well known in the world as you are, and has your wealth and beauty would be hard to stay hidden even in London."

Then, he turned toward Tom and said, "You have to be one of the luckiest men in the world to have such a wonderful wife."

Tom replied, "It's hard for me to believe that I was lucky enough to have such a wonderful wife."

The Captain said, "I'm certainly pretty lucky to have two very nice people like Jenny and Uranus that are willing to help my officer's son with his medical expenses in Switzerland."

Jenny asked, "Do you have any idea what kind of money your officer is going to need to pay for his son's medical expenses?"

"No, I don't, but just to get started they are asking about two hundred and fifty thousand pounds. The reason it's so much is because they have been working on this drug that they want to use to treat him and it has some type of compounds they have been working with to try to find out which one of the ingredients may work best to cure the boy."

Jenny asked, "Captain, what kind of medical problems is the boy having?"

"That's part of the problem. He has so many; one, he can hardly digest food and then along with that it affects his arms and legs. He can hardly use his arms to pick up things and he can't stand or walk. He's about ten years old and only weighs about forty-five pounds and is only about three and a half feet tall."

"The doctors think all of these problems are caused by his brain and they think if they can find the right combination of meds that would save the boy and let him grow to the right weight and height, he would be able to use his legs and arms."

Jenny said "Well,, I would be willing to provide the two hundred fifty thousand pounds to help the boy."

Then Uranus added, "I would be willing to put up the same amount, since I know from my own experience that doctors always under-estimate how much it's going to cost to have any experimental drugs to try on the boy."

Captain Hayes replied, "Wow, I'm sure the boy's mother and father are going to be so pleased to have this help for their son."

Jenny asked, "Who should we write the checks to?"

The Captain replied, "I don't know, but I can ask the boy's father, so we have the right name on the checks."

Uranus said, "OK, Captain Hayes. I'll tell you what I'll do. I'll write my check and leave the name of the company or doctor that it's going to be made out to blank. Then, when you get the right name, you can put it on the check. Is that OK with you, Captain?"

The Captain replied, "Well, I would like to know the name of the person that's going to be doing the research that you two are going to be helping. I wouldn't want a check for a quarter million pounds lying around without having who it's going to be paid to, not even in the police department."

Uranus smiled and said, "Hayes, you have just broken my faith in the police department."

The four of them laughed, before Captain Hayes retorted, "Well, I guess you could just make the check out to me. Then I could just retire in Spain where it's really hard to get much help from their folks in the police department to try to find someone wanted in another country."

"That brought laughter from all four of them."

When the laughter ceased, Uranus said, "OK, Captain Hayes. How about you just call me when you know who the check should be made out to and I'll stop by your office and give you the check."

The Captain replied, "Much better idea. I know the boy's parents will greatly appreciate both of you helping,"

With that being said, Tom asked, "Uranus, have we ever met or talked on the phone because your name is so familiar."

"No, I'm sure we have never met before or talked on the phone."

Torn replied, "Well, I'm sure I spoke to someone on the phone recently who said his name was Uranus."

"Well, Torn, that's a popular name where I come from. I guess it's kind of like Bob or Torn where you come from."

"Thanks, Uranus, I just had to ask."

"No problem, it seems like someone who has that name is in trouble with the police all the time. I've been questioned several times in Europe due to my first name before they realize they have got the wrong Uranus."

"Thanks, for the information. I'm sorry to hear you have a problem with the police sometimes due to your first name. I recently got a call from a man with that name threatening to kill me."

"Trust me, it wasn't me."

"I'm glad to hear that."

Then Tom laughed. This made the rest of the folks laugh.

CHAPTER TWENTY-ONE

SO THERE ARE MORE THAN ONE URANUS IN LONDON

Tom said, "You know, Captain Hayes, this case gets to be more and more of a puzzle every day."

"Well, Tom, frankly, I'd never heard of anyone that was named Uranus until I met Uranus Al-Sadr. He's been someone that I've called on several times to help provide money to several of our officers because of health problems for them, their wives or kids."

Tom said, "He's a lot different than I expected him to be. He seems more English than someone from the Middle East."

"Probably, it's because he was born here and has lived in London all of his life. He graduated from Oxford as the top honor student in his class and has never lived anywhere but London. His father and mother moved to London before Uranus was born, so he was born here and has always been an Englishman."

"His grandfather was one of the first to own land where oil was found in the Middle East and after Uranus grew up and took over the family business, he diversified the family holdings into many other businesses. Apparently, the family just keeps getting richer and richer every year. That's why he is so quick to help so many people."

Tom then said, "Well, I don't think he's the one who called and threatened to kill me for killing his brother."

Captain Hayes added, "As far as I know. Uranus never had a brother. Only a couple of sisters, both who married Englishmen and they all live here in London."

Tom replied, "Sounds like a pretty good life for him and all of his family."

"Well, Tom, I'd say they are not involved with terrorists, that's for sure, and they have no reason to be."

Tom told Captain Hayes he and Jenny would be going back to their hotel, since he never confided to the Captain that they were actually staying at their CIA apartment.

Benny was waiting at the curb with their Rolls and ready to take them anywhere they might wish to go.

Benny saw them coming out of the police station. So, he got out of the Rolls and opened the door for Jenny, then quickly went to the other side of the car to open the door for Tom.

No matter how many times Tom told him that it was all right, that he could open his own car door, it wasn't all right with Benny. That was his job, so now, Tom made sure he let Benny open his door.

After they were in the car and had their seat belts on, Benny asked them where they wished to go.

Jenny replied, "Los Angeles."

Benny wanted to play along and asked, "Should I go to Heathrow or to the Queen Mary's docking space?"

Tom replied, "You're pretty quick asking questions of how Jenny wanted to go home."

Benny said, "I just think Miss Jenny is really ready to go home, sir."

Tom said, "If we go home, what are you going to do without us? You know you will be missing us and we will sure be missing you, Benny."

"Well, I will certainly be missing both of you."

"You won't miss us for a little while longer, because tonight we're just going to go back to the CIA Headquarters."

"Yes, sir, Mr. Tom," he said, as Benny pulled the Rolls away from the curb and began to drive in the general direction of the CIA Building."

Before they had been driving more than a few blocks, Benny said, "Mr. Tom, I think that little black car is following us."

Tom asked, "What makes you think so, Benny?"

"After we'd gone a few blocks after leaving the police station, I saw that little black car made a U-turn in the middle of the block and began staying very close behind us. If I made a turn, it made a turn and then it continued to stay not far behind us."

"I'll tell you what, Benny. At the next traffic signal, make a right turn and as soon as you can, find a parking space that you can pull our car over to the curb and see if he stops behind us."

"Yes, sir, Mr. Tom.

Benny had only a couple of minutes before he began signaling for a right turn and the little black car also begin signaling for a right turn.

Tom said, "When you get to the corner, keep signaling for that right turn. Then, speed up and go straight, then, pull over to the curb and park."

Tom took out his automatic and checked to be sure it was ready to fire. Benny did as Tom told him. He blew through the intersection and pulled the Rolls quickly over to the curb. The little black car did the same thing, except it kept going past the parked limo and then, stopped and pulled over to the curb about seventy-five feet in front of the Rolls.

Two men jumped out of the car, one on one side of the car and one on the other side and began coming toward the Rolls with weapons drawn in their hands.

Tom said, "Benny, drive as fast as you can directly toward the man on the outside of that car and I'll take care of the man on the inside of that car."

Suddenly, the men saw the Rolls with spinning wheels pulling away from the curb and, at the same time, Tom moved over to where Jenny was sitting and quickly pushed her down on the seat.

Then Tom pushed the button to lower the window and fired a shot at the man closest to the Rolls and down he went.

That happened at the same time as Benny pulled the Rolls farther away from the curb and struck the other man that was coming after them with a gun with the car's bumper. the man hit the fender and down he went.

This all happened so quickly that neither man actually got a shot off at them.

By this time Benny had the Rolls going down the street as if nothing had happened at all.

Jenny finally got sit to back up and said, "Did you have to push me down so hard, just because some man was coming at me with a gun? I could have probably shot him myself."

Tom replied, "Sorry, my love. Instinct took over my body and it caused me to react as I normally would. So I just had to shoot that man coming at you with his gun. Sorry, I'll try to do better next time."

"OK, Tom. I'll forgive you this time, but try to keep control of your instinct the next time."

"Yes, dear."

"I guess I should call Captain Hayes and tell him where those two bodies are."

Jenny replied, "I guess you should, so he knows you still have people trying to kill us here in London."

Tom took out his cell phone and called Captain Hayes and when his call was answered, Tom heard, "This is Captain Hayes, how may I help you?"

"Captain, this is Tom Parker and I have to tell you that a few minutes after we left the station. We had two men in a little black car following us and we tried to get away from them. Benny made several turns to try to shake them, but to no avail.

"So, I had him stop on a deserted street to see what they would do. Then they got out of their car with guns drawn and started back to the Rolls. I moved Jenny over on the seat and shot one of the men."

"Then I had our driver, Benny. to try to drive around the other man with a gun, but the car hit the man with our bumper." "Benny checked to see if he needed medical attention, but he was already dead.

"Captain, I'm going to give my phone to Benny so he can tell you where these men's bodies are located. Do we need to come back to the station and fill out a report about this or can we wait until tomorrow?"

"No, Tom, you don't have to come back tonight to fill out a report. I'm pretty sure both of those two dead men will still be dead tomorrow morning."

"Thank you, Captain, here's Benny. We'll see you in the morning."

Tom handed the phone to Benny and Benny quickly gave the Captain the street information of where the men's bodies were.

Benny soon had them back to the CIA Building and up to the floor where their apartment was located.

Tom told Benny he should just stay the night in the other bedroom that they had in their apartment, but Benny told him, no, he needed to go home to be able to get ready for work tomorrow."

Then Tom said, "Benny, what would you think about bringing enough clothes and your shaving things, toothbrush and any medications that you know you need to be able to stay a week with us."

"Mr. Tom, if you want me to be here so that I can be ready to take you anywhere night and day. I would be happy to do that."

"Benny, the way things are going here, I think that would be a very good idea, if it's not too much to ask of you."

"No, sir, Mr. Tom. I'd do anything for you and Miss Jenny, you are the finest people. I've ever worked for."

"Well, if you don't tell my wife what I'm going to tell you." (Jenny was seated right beside him.)

"I want you to know, you're the best driver we have ever had. That's including my wife's driver, who's also our butler. He and his wife have been taking care of Jenny since she was born. But it's getting to be too much for both of them."

Tom then said, "If you would like to keep working for us after we finish our assignment here in London. I would like for you to go home with us and to become our full-time driver in America."

"Well, I have would have to think about that. I don't know if I could get permission to go to America. I have a passport, but I've only used it to travel to places in Europe, when I was working driving cars in movies or driving race cars."

Tom replied, "If you have a valid passport. I'll take care of everything else."

"Yes, sir, I do have a valid passport."

Tom said, "Sorry, I didn't even ask you if you would like to go to America or if you had a wife, girlfriend or family here in England that you wouldn't want to move away from."

"Sorry, Benny, sometimes I just get carried away when I want something to happen.

Then, I just fail to ask what they might like."

"Well, I don't have anyone that's still living; my grandmother raised me after my folks were killed in a car accident. I was just two years old.

"My grandmother died three years ago and I just live in a rented room on the other side of London. I never had a girl friend, because I was too shy to ask any of the girls that I liked. So I never dated."

"I always loved cars, that's why I got to be a pretty good driver and I got work in the movies and racing. Then, I became a chauffeur and I've been passing up doing movies and racing ever since then."

"OK, Benny, I want you to bring all of your things and move into our other bedroom and if we have to leave here and go back to the hotel. You will just live there near us until we leave for America, OK?"

"In America, you will be living in our big house in Beverly Hills, California, if that's OK with you."

"Yes, sir, Mr. Tom. Tomorrow I'll bring all of my things with me to be ready to go to America whenever you are finished in London."

"Great! Good night, and I'll see you in the morning and, thank you, Benny, for wanting to keep working for us."

"Benny, from now on you have a family, we may not be the best family, but we'll always be there for you."

Tom could see tears in Benny's eyes as he heard Benny say, "Thank you, Mr. Tom. I'll see you in the morning."

As Benny drove away, Jenny said, "Tom, I'm so proud of you. That's one of the nicest things that you may have ever done."

Tom retorted, "Well, I married you when you were a poor widow, that was pretty nice, don't you think?"

"Damn nice, and I had a poor little girl at the time and you took both of us in."

"OK, so you took me in. Because I was a poor boy that loved you just for who you were. Isn't that right?"

"Damn right, so let's get to bed before somebody else tries to kill us or you add another person to our family."

All had been said, as Jenny was laughing like mad.

CHAPTER TWENTY-TWO

WHAT POSSIBLY COULD HAPPEN NEXT TO TOM & JENNY?

The next morning, Tom heard his telephone ringing before he got out of bed.

He took his phone off the small table next to their bed and said, "Tom Parker,' and then Tom heard a man say, "I'm getting tired of you killing my men. So I guess I'll have to take care of you myself."

Tom replied, "Well, I hope you're a lot better than those two clowns you sent last night."

"Don't worry. I will be!"

"I'd say you're the one that better be worried. How many of your men have I had to kill since I've been in London? I can't remember. I need to know, so I can log them on my kill sheet."

"You'll never get to add them, because you'll be dead." Then the phone went dead.

Then Tom said, "Jenny, that no good guy has called me again just to tell me he's going to kill me. So I better have breakfast, because I don't want to die on an empty stomach."

"Tom, please don't say that."

"Sorry, but it's the truth. I'm really hungry this morning.

"Jenny got up and made one stop into the bathroom then into the kitchen and she found someone had stocked up some food in the fridge. They had bacon and eggs. Even some fruit in a small container. She also found coffee, bread, strawberry jam and butter.

So, she began frying bacon and then the eggs. Then after Tom was out of the shower, he got dressed and begin making toast and coffee.

By the time Jenny had the bacon and eggs ready. Tom was buttering the toast and the coffee was just finishing making in the large coffee maker.

They soon sat down at the kitchen table as Tom was pouring the coffee. Tom even had put out the cream for Jenny's coffee.

Jenny said their morning prayer before they had breakfast and she asked God to take special care of Tom during their stay in London and protect him as He had been doing all during Tom's life.

Tom thanked Jenny for her prayer and said, "Let's enjoy this wonderful breakfast that you made for us."

Making breakfast wasn't something that she normally did. Tom didn't even know if she knew how to cook, because she always had people to do those kinds of things for her.

As they were eating their breakfast Tom said to Jenny, "You know sweetheart. I had no idea that you even knew how to cook. I knew you always had people to do those things. I want you to know. I'm so proud of you. You prepared a wonderful breakfast for us."

"Tom, I'll have you know, my parents insisted that I learn how to do everything to run a home and how to do them: cooking, doing the laundry, ironing, sewing and even how to shop for groceries and what it took to clean the home."

"My mother told me, "If you don't know how to take care of the home and know how to cook, how will you know if your staff is doing a good job?"

"The other thing about that learning, I always had the best people that did each of those things to teach me. So, I was, of course, a very good student for them, just like it was in school and at the university. I was always the best student in my classes."

"OK, my love. No wonder I love you so much you know almost everything."

"No, Tom. I have no idea how I am going to keep you alive when so many people are trying to kill you."

"The same old way I've been doing it for most of my life. I'll be ready for whoever tries to kill me or you."

"OK, just keep doing a good job of it."

"I'll do my best."

Not too long after they finished breakfast, Benny arrived with all of his personal things, including his passport.

Tom looked over his British Passport and saw it was OK and wouldn't expire for five more years. So, it should be no problem for Benny to arrive in America.

Benny didn't have very many things to take with him when they left to go back to the States. He only had his clothes and a few pictures that he brought in a paper sack.

Tom said, "Before we leave London, we need to get you a new suitcase and something to carry your pictures in. Maybe we can get you a small hard-back briefcase to put your pictures in, so they don't get lost or bent up."

"Thank you, Mr. Tom, that would be appreciated."

"One other thing, please just call me Tom. I think you are talking to someone else when you call me Mr. Tom. I'm just Tom and Jenny, or if you feel better. you can call Jenny. Miss Jenny, if you're more comfortable doing that."

"Thank you, Mr. Tom, I mean Tom. I prefer to call Mrs. Parker, Miss Jenny, if that's OK?"

"That's fine, Benny, I understand that's from your training."

"OK ,Tom."

"Good, we've got that settled. Now, I have to figure out what we need to do today. So why don't you go in the kitchen and have some tea or coffee. There may be something left in the kitchen for you to eat. If so, please help yourself."

"OK, Tom, when you're ready to go somewhere. I'll in be in my room or in the kitchen."

"Thanks, Benny. I'll see you later."

Then, Tom heard his phone ringing again and thought, you've got to be kidding who's calling me now to tell me they are going to kill me.

Tom answered his phone, "Tom Parker."

Tom heard, "Good morning, Tom. This is Blake Pearson and I was wondering if you could have lunch with me today at my borrowed home. I wanted to thank you for saving my wife's life."

"I certainly would love to join you for lunch, but I don't think I'm the one who saved her. It was Jenny. She's the one who had the tracking device that let us find them."

"Well, Suri told me that you were the reason Jenny had that device, since you were the one who made her have it put in her shoulder."

"I guess that's the truth but nobody can made my wife do anything she doesn't want to do. I might suggest you have your folks put one into Suri's shoulder so you can keep track of her."

"Great idea, but I don't think we have enough satellites to keep track of Suri like America has to keep track of Jenny."

"Also, Suri told me that Jenny said she agreed to let them to put that tracking device in her shoulder because you were never going to shut up about it, until she let them put that device in."

"OK, Blake, that is probably true. So, what time would you like me to come for lunch?"

"Let's be old-fashioned, let's make it noon."

"All right, Blake. I'll see you at twelve o'clock."

Jenny came into the living room just as Tom was putting his phone back into his phone case and asked, "Who was that on the phone?"

"Blake Pearson. He invited me to lunch today at noon at his "Borrowed Home," as he calls it."

"Tom, you know he and Suri are really fine people don't you think?"

"I certainly do and this idea that he would help Russia against America is just plain nuts."

"Good, does that mean we can go home now and you can tell the President that there's no reason to think he's helping Russia in anyway?"

"Not quite, we still don't know who keeps trying to kill me or you, and until we do that, I'm not leaving London."

"I was afraid you would say that. So, go have your lunch with the Prime Minster and if you see Suri, please tell her I was thinking about her."

CHAPTER TWENTY-THREE

TOM THINKS HE KNOWS WHO IS TRYING TO KILL HIM

Tom told Benny that he was ready for him to drive him over to the Prime Minister's home for a lunch meeting.

As they traveled along, Tom asked Benny to drive by the Claridge Hotel on the way to the Prime Minister's home and to pull into the driveway as if he was going to park and pick someone up.

Benny did as Tom asked him to do, but before he drove into the driveway, Tom laid down on the back seat of the limo.

Benny stopped for a few seconds then Tom sat back up and told Benny to drive on toward the Prime Minister's Home.

Benny pulled out of the hotel driveway and after they had go only a few blocks, Benny said, "Tom, I think your idea worked, there's a black car following us now."

"Benny, can you tell how many people are in that car?"

"I can only see two men in the front seat."

"OK, Benny, just keep driving to the Prime Minister's house and let's see what they do when you pull up in front of the Prime Minister's house."

Several minutes later, Benny made a left turn onto the street that the Prime Minister's house was on and parked in front of the house.

The black car made a left turn onto the same street, but when they saw the guards outside of the Prime Minister's home, they drove on down the street and turned around.

The guards recognized Tom, since he had been there recently and they showed him into the house.

Tom asked if it was all right if his car was parked in front of the house and they told him it was OK as long as the driver stayed with the car.

As Tom was going into the house, he saw the black car drive slowly back by the house then turned back onto the same street and direction that they had just come from.

Benny took his phone out and as the car drove past him, he took pictures of the car and the two men in the car.

When Tom got into the house he was soon met by Prime Minster Blake Pearson who said, "Come on into the kitchen with me, because I decided we were going to have a cozy place to have our lunch."

Tom replied, "That sounds good to me."

Blake said, "Well, Tom, I'm sure you know that when you have a job like mine, you have so many lunches and dinners that you have to go to and they always expect me to give a little performance because it's part of my job."

"However, sometimes you have someone you feel like they are a real friend and it would be nice to just relax and enjoy your friend's company. That's the way I feel when I'm with you."

"Well, Blake, that's the nicest thing anyone has said to me in a long time and I'm sure, given the opportunity, we could be best friends. However,,in my case that doesn't seem like a very good thing for you. For all of my best friends soon get killed and I certainly don't want that happening to you, so, could we just agree to become very close friends?"

Blake started laughing and said, "OK, Tom, we will never be best friends, just very close friends because my wife wouldn't like it if I got killed."

"You've got a deal, my friend. We are just very close friends. I might add, I don't think the people in the UK would like it if you got killed because of me either."

"Well, some of my opposition members in the Parliament would probably cheer loudly."

"I doubt that your opposition members would cheer. They would be afraid your party would pick someone worse than you."

That made Blake laugh and he said, "Surely, they couldn't find anyone worse than me. If you don't believe it, just ask one of my opposition members. They would tell you they couldn't get anyone worse than me."

Just then a very pretty young lady came in and said, "Sir, I have to remind you that you need to have your lunch, since you have a meeting in White Hall at two thirty."

Blake immediately stopped laughing and said, "Thank you, Thelma."

He then said, "Tom, this young lady is my secretary's secretary. She's the one who keeps all of us making and keeping our appointments on time and she generally tries to watch over us."

"Thelma, this gentleman is the famous General Tom Parker, who saved Suri's life, and Tom' this is Thelma Baxter, my rigid time scheduler."

Thelma smiled and said, "How do you do ,General Parker?"

Tom returned her smile and said, "Tell me, how you keep all of your charges making it to all of their meetings every day."

"Oh, it's not easy with this one, he gets so many meetings scheduled every day."

Tom said, "Well, I guess you will just have to keep after him to be sure he gets to where ever he is scheduled to be."

Blake said, "Thank you again, Thelma. I guess Tom and I have to eat our lunch instead of having a conversation."

With that said, Thelma smiled again, turned around and walked out of the room.

Blake then said, "See, Tom, these people won't even let me have any free time to enjoy lunch with my friends and have a few laughs."

"Tom, I do have to thank you again for saving Suri and you know America is the UK's younger brother don't you?"

"He's the one who's bigger, stronger and has all of the new toys, like electronic devices in their shoulders. That way dad can always find them wherever they are on this earth."

Tom just smiled and said nothing more, but in a way, what Blake was saying was true.

America was younger and stronger than the UK in today's world.

Blake and Tom ate their lunch and talked and talked, until it was time for Blake to go to his meeting. Then, before Blake left, the two men embraced and Blake said "I wished we could have more time to talk and be together."

Tom replied, "Yes, I feel the same way. It's been a long time since I had a best friend. Now I have one, just don't tell anyone. I don't want to lose you."

Blake went off to his meeting and Tom returned to his car and told Benny to take him back to the CIA Building.

When Tom was in his car, he called Captain Hayes and asked him to see what information they had on a young woman by the name of Thelma Baxter who works in Prime Minister Blake Pearson's office.

Before they got back to the CIA Building, Captain Hayes called Tom.

He said, This is what we have on file about Thelma Baxter. She works in the office of the Prime Minster. She is a graduate of Oxford with a degree in social science. Her parents were both professors at Oxford. Now both are deceased, they were killed in a car wreck in Turkey a couple of years ago.

"She had a boy friend for a couple of years now, but as far as we know, she has no plans on getting married soon. Although they don't live together, they are thought to be together most of the time when they are not working."

"He is from Iran; his name is Armand Tyrus and although he was born in the UK and his mother is English, he was educated in Finland and then was a graduate of Oxford with a degree in political science and he has UK Citizenship. He and Baxter were class mates; however they didn't date when they were attending Oxford. He lives full-time in London and works at the Iranian Embassy. What he does there, we don't know."

Tom said, "Thank you, Captain, for the information. I have a hunch he may be the one that's supplying information to the hit squad that's been trying to kill me ever since I got to London."

Captain Hayes asked, "Do you think he has any idea what these people are trying to do?"

"You know, that's a good question and that's an interesting question for Thelma Baxter. Because I'm pretty sure she's the one that giving information to Armand, and he's passing it on to the hit squad."

"You know, Captain, maybe he doesn't have any idea what these people are trying to do either, and wouldn't that be interesting?"

Captain Hayes said, "You know, I think I should just have both of them brought in to the police station and have the two of us questioning them. What do you think about that?"

"I think that's a very good idea, but I don't think they should have any idea that they are both being questioned."

"Yes, I agree. I'll have both of them brought in, but not let the other one know we have both of them."

Tom said, "You will have to be careful, because if the Prime Minster thinks you are harassing them, he's going to be on your case, because I know he thinks highly of Ms. Baxter and in the few minutes that I saw her, it would be easy to do."

"She's a very pretty young woman who appears to be very dedicated to her job of making sure the Prime Minster is where he is supposed to be for every scheduled meeting."

Captain Hayes replied, "OK, Tom we will be very careful with both of them, but also they won't know we are talking with the other one."

"Great, Captain, however, I do want to be there when you speak with them, but of course I don't want to be in the interrogation room. I need to watch their reaction while you are questioning them."

"OK, Tom, I'll let you know when we have picked them up and, of course, they won't have any idea that the other one has been picked up. I'll call you when we have them en route to the police headquarters."

"Sounds good, I'll see you very soon."

Forty five minutes later, Tom got a call from Captain Hayes telling him that they had picked up both Baxter and Tyrus and they would soon be at police headquarters.

Tom again stated how important it was to be sure these two people didn't know the other one had been taken in to be questioned.

The Captain assured Tom they will not know the other one was in the police station to be questioned.

The officers took Thelma into Room One and Armand into Room Two. They had no way of knowing that the other one had been brought in to the police station. They just couldn't understand why they had brought into a police station.

Captain Hayes would be questioning Thelma first. When he entered Room One, he said, "Miss Baxter, my name is Captain Hayes with Scotland Yard and I am sure you are wondering why you are here.

"So, I am going to tell you why you are here. I know you keep track of all of the meetings that many people have in the Prime Minister's office every day, including the Prime Minister's meetings."

"However, General Tom Parker and his wife have been working in London and this couple have been attacked several times during their stay and have been very come close to been killed."

"Thelma said, "I'm sorry, I didn't know that. I did know that Mrs. Parker had been kidnapped along with Mrs. Pearson and she was the one who had some type of tracking device that made it possible for them to be rescued."

"That's true, however, before that, and then again yesterday, Mrs. Parker was attacked and only quick work by group of her employees saved her from either being captured or killed."

"So, what does that have to do with me? Thelma asked."

"Well, that's why you have been brought to Scotland Yards. You are one of the few people in the British Government that knows a lot about government officials' appointments, such as the Prime Minister's."

"I don't understand what that has to do with Mrs. Parker and her husband being attacked. Just because I know where the people that I work with are going?"

"Have you ever told your boy friend, Armand Tyrus, any information about things like that, you know, like where Mrs. Pearson is going?"

"Well, I'm sure I have. We talk a lot on the phone."

"Has he ever asked you about where the Prime Minster or his wife is going?"

"I don't know, maybe he has. Are you trying to say he has something to do with Mrs. Pearson and Mrs. Parker being kidnapped?"

"I don't know, do you think he might have had something to do with them being kidnapped?"

"I didn't say he had anything to do with them being kidnapped. Are you trying to put words in my mouth?"

"No, Thelma. I'm just trying to find out if you think it's possible that things that you may have told Armand may have been connected to the kidnapping of Mrs. Pearson and Mrs. Parker and the attacks on General and Mrs. Parker during their stay in London."

"Why are you asking me these questions, do you have any proof that Armand had anything to do with these things?"

"We are just trying to find out if you have ever provided him with any information regarding where General and Mrs. Parker are since they have been in London. We don't think you have had anything to do with the people who have tried to kill them or kidnap Mrs. Pearson and Mrs. Parker. However, inadvertently, you may have provided information that let these people do these things."

"Captain Hayes, do I need an attorney?"

"I don't think you do, but I am trying to find out if somehow during your conversations with Armand, if there was information about when and how the meeting of Mrs. Pearson and Mrs. Parker was going to happen."

"Captain, do you think Armand had anything to do with them being kidnapped?"

"I don't know if he did. I only know that someone had to know when and how they were going to be together to be able to kidnap them."

Thelma said, "Well, I think I did say something to Armand about them having lunch that day and that Mrs. Pearson would be picking up Mrs. Parker at her hotel."

"But, I can't see how that could have caused them to be kidnapped by those awful people."

"Thelma, only if Armand contacted the people who kidnapped them to let them know that when Mrs. Pearson and her driver were picking up Mrs. Parker at her hotel."

"Then, all they had to do was to watch for Mrs. Pearson's car stopping at the Claridge Hotel and picking up Mrs. Parker, and then they could kidnap both of them."

"Captain Hayes, do you really think Armand had anything to do with the kidnapping of Mrs. Pearson and that other lady?"

"Well, it seems very likely that he did. Where he works caused us to question if he just a very nice, good-looking young man that became involved with a very beautiful young woman who works handling lots of the Prime Minister's and his staff's appointments, as well as with his wife's."

"Is it love that he has for you or is it that he could be using you for information about what goes on in the Prime Minister's office? We don't have an answer for that question."

"What do you think, Thelma?"

"Well, I love him and he says he loves me, and he certainly acts like he does."

"Thelma, I'm going to have an officer take you home and when you talk with Armand, please don't tell him that the police picked you up to talk about your relationship with him."

"Do your best to act as you always have with him. I hope you understand that we don't have enough information yet to decide if he is really involved in the kidnapping of our First Lady and her friend or not. But we believe he is involved in our investigation of the kidnapping and may be involved with the attempts on the Parker's lives."

The Captain told the officer who had been in the interrogation room with them to please have Ms. Baxter taken home.

CHAPTER TWENTY-FOUR

ARE THEY GETTING ANY CLOSER TO KNOWING WHO'S AFTER TOM PARKER?

CAPTAIN Hayes asked Tom what he thought about his talk with Thelma Baxter.

Tom said, "Well, I thought Ms. Baxter was shocked to think she might have helped to have Mrs. Pearson kidnapped. I'm sure she never considered that telling Armand Tyrus about where and when Mrs. Pearson was having lunch would cause her to be kidnapped."

"Also, I think she maybe busy thinking about what else she may have told Armand about things at work that might have helped the people behind the kidnapping to do other things that may have hurt her country."

"You may be right, General Parker. I think she was surprised to have someone thinking that she may have done something that might hurt her country or harm Mrs. Pearson.'"

"Well, let's see what Armand Tyrus has to say when you question him. Captain, how about you just calling me Tom, OK?"

"OK, if you're happy with that. I will Tom."

"Good, let's hear Armand answers."

Tom left the room and Captain Hayes had Armand brought into the room."

Captain Hayes said, "Is your name Armand Tyrus, were you born in London?"

Armand answered, "Yes sir, my name is Armand Tyrus and I was born in London."

"Armand, where do you work?"

"I work at the Finland Embassy."

"What do you do at the Finland Embassy?"

"I work with people who want to travel to Finland."

"What is required for people to travel to Finland?"

"They have to have a Finland Visa."

"Is that hard to get?"

"It depends on what country they come from and the purpose of their trip."

"If you were from the United States would that be harder to get a Visa ,for example, than if you were from Germany?"

"No, it wouldn't be hard to get a Visa for either one of those countries."

"Do you date, Thelma Baxter?'

"Why would you ask me about who I date, you know I'm a British citizen. So, I can date anyone I want to, don't you think?"

"We think you date her to get information about people in the government, like who they meet with and when and where."

"Did she tell you that I did that? I date her because I love her and want to marry her?"

"By marrying her, then you could get even more information about things that were going on in the British Government, isn't that the real reason you want to marry her?"

"You're crazy man. I want a lawyer. I'm not going to answer any more of your questions."

"OK, do you have an attorney or would we have to help you find one? Either way, since its late Friday night we probably wouldn't be able to contact one. Do you have an attorney?"

"No."

"Well, for us to get you an attorney, we probably would have to wait until sometime Monday morning."

"So, in the meantime, we will just have to keep you locked up until we can help you get an attorney."

"Wait a minute, maybe I could just answer your questions. I don't want to be locked up for the weekend."

Since Tom could hear and see the questioning of Armand, he thought Captain Jack Hayes of Scotland Yard was a pretty smart cookie to be able to get Armand to agree to keep answering questions.

"OK, let's see if we can get through my questions for you, OK?"

"OK."

"Did you ask Ms. Baxter if she knew if Suri Pearson would be meeting with Jenny Parker?"

"I don't know. Is it important?"

"Yes, it's kind of important."

"Well, I may have. I don't know. I ask Thelma a lot of questions because she meets so many important people."

"Do you know that Mrs. Pearson and Mrs. Parker were kidnapped soon after they met to go to lunch and it was only a miracle that they were both rescued?"

"Well, it was pretty hard not to know about them being kidnapped and getting rescued. Since that' was the only news on the radio and television all day long."

"Armand, were you one of the kidnappers of these two women?"

"I never kidnapped anybody, much less those two women."

"Do you know that because you told the people who were involved in the kidnapping of Mrs. Pearson and Mrs. Parker when they were going to lunch, that you can be charged with the crime, just like the ones who actually took these two women?"

"Wait a minute. All I ever did was to tell people that I work with at the Embassy that these ladies were going to lunch."

"Did you tell them what time they were going to lunch and where they were going to pick up Mrs. Parker?"

"I don't remember, maybe I did. I'm not sure."

"Did you know Mrs. Parker was a CIA Agent?"

"No, I had no idea. All I knew was that she was here with her husband who's a CIA Agent and he had killed several people."

"I heard he's a very bad man, he likes to kill people."

"You know, Armand, I think I need to hold you to keep you safe from your friends. Because of what you told me about you telling them about when Mrs. Pearson and Mrs. Parker were going to meet, that let them know when to kidnap those two women."

"Right now you are facing serious charges of the kidnapping of these women. However, if you agree to testify against the person or persons you gave the information to, I can get you off with only probation and no jail time."

"OK, my mommy would not be happy if I went to jail."

"No, I'm sure she wouldn't, nor would Thelma Baxter, because I know she likes you a lot."

"I do have to tell you that I'm going to have to put you in protective custody to be certain you aren't killed before the trial of these men begin."

"What does that mean?"

"It means you will be staying in a home and that you will have to remain there until the trial is over. That's just to keep you safe. You will be able to talk with your mother on the telephone and maybe with Ms. Baxter and you may get to see and visit with both of them."

"After I talk with Thelma Baxter, I'll explain you didn't know these people were going to kidnap Mrs. Pearson and Mrs. Parker. You didn't know they planned to kidnap them, did you?"

"No, I had no idea they were going to do that."

"Then you should be all right with Ms. Baxter because I know she likes you a lot."

"We are going to have to move fast to catch all of the people involved in this and their efforts to kill General and Mrs. Parker."

"He deserves to die for all of the people he's killed."

"I don't think he is the awful person you think he is. I understand that he's only been involved in killing people when they have been trying to kill him or his wife or on the battlefield."

"My people tell me he's killed many people just to show how tough he is."

"Armand, I think you have been told the wrong stories by the wrong people. They hate everything that a man like Tom Parker stands for."

"He's for protecting the people who can't protect themselves and for protecting countries like the United States and England."

"I can tell you one thing, he's tough, but from what I know, he would only kill when he was protecting someone who couldn't protect themselves or his own life."

"Maybe I'm wrong, but I've only heard he just likes to kill people."

"Armand, how would like to meet him to see for yourself if he just likes to kill people?"

"I don't know. He might kill me just because my folks were from Finland and I work in their Embassy."

"How about you finding out for yourself, so you really know something about the man your people have told you about, to see for yourself if he is that bad?"

"I guess that would be all right."

"OK, I'm going to have you meet him right now."

"Do you mean here, right now?"

"Yes, that's what I mean. Tom, please come in to meet Armand Tyrus."

Armand slumped down in his chair and waited to die right there.

Tom came into the room and said, "Armand, I'm very glad to get to meet you and to let you know I have no ill feelings toward you. What I would like to tell you is that the people you have been working with have been using you to help them undermine your real home country, England."

"You don't have to believe me, but stop and think about the kind of questions they ask you. Like, do you know if your girl friend Thelma knows if Mrs. Pearson is going to meet with the wife of that CIA Agent, Tom Parker, while they are in London?"

"Armand, think back to all kinds of questions they ask you that could help some way to hurt your fellow countrymen, you know the English people. Stop and think, you're not from Finland."

"Your parents moved here to get away from what was happening in their old country. Not all people from Finland are bad people, and I'm sorry to say this, but the ones that are running the country right now are not wonderful people."

Tom continued, "I know I'm not the nicest guy in this world, but I am a highly trained military man from West Point. We are highly trained to protect the United States of America from all enemies, foreign or domestic, and I have dedicated my life to doing exactly that, and that's what I'm doing in London."

Tom then asked, "Who do you work for at the Embassy?"

"Ambassador Zig Klebe, he's a very nice man, and there are other people who work in Security that I'm not so sure about what their names are, but they always seem to be having troubles of some kind."

Tom said, "Armand, do you know since my wife and I have been in London we've been attacked several times by what I thought was foreign agents, but in truth I think they are people that are primarily drug dealers. However, I think they may be working through the Finland Embassy and that they have taken control of the drug trade in London."

Armand asked, "Why do you think these people having been trying to kill you?"

"Because they know I'm involved in looking into some things that our local CIA Agents have been thinking; things like the Prime Minster has been involved in with foreign countries. This is not true at all. But these people know who I am and they are concerned that I will get involved in messing up their business."

"If their business turns out to be dealing drugs, trust me, I am going to mess up their business, with your and the London's Police Department's help. They have tried to kill me and my wife ever since we arrived in London."

"Armand tell me about the people who work at the Embassy and what department they work in and what their jobs are?"

Armand said, "Well, there are several people who work at the Embassy and I certainly don't know all of their names, just their jobs. The Embassy has different departments with a man in charge of each department: Security: Visa Applications: Visa Approval: Customer Service: Collector of the fees: They all work for the Ambassador."

"I don't really know all of the names of these people, because I primarily just worked for Ambassador Zig Klebe."

"What did you do for the Ambassador?"

"Well, it was more public relations. I would go with him to meetings and I helped him with English during these meetings. We've met with several British departments and it seemed like he was always trying to get funds for various projects. He said he was trying to get it done for Finland."

"Did you ever see large amounts of money lying around when you were in his office?"

"Sometimes, if I was in his office late on a Friday night, I saw a lot of money lying on his desk."

"Did he ever say anything about this money?"

"No, and I never asked about it. When you work in the Finland Embassy, you never ask too many questions."

Tom said, "Captain Hayes, I think you should make arrangements for Armand to be placed in a safe house for the night before it gets any later."

Captain Hayes said, "Yes, it is getting pretty late. I'11 make arrangements for two of my officers to take Armand to a safe house right now."

The Captain left to contact officers to take Armand to a safe house.

Tom asked, can you tell me the names of some of the people who are in charge of the different departments at the Embassy?"

"Yes, I can, but because their first names are so hard for the English workers they use names that are easier for the people living and working here to pronounce. Charlie is in charge of working with the local government officials: John is head of Security, Steve takes care of the building maintenance, Evert takes care of the filing of records, including recording deaths and births of Finland's citizens living in the United Kingdom. Last, you have Zig, who's in charge of Finland's Embassy, you know, he's the big guy."

Tom said, "That's a funny thing you said, calling the Finland Ambassador, the big guy. I've recently heard an informant calling the head of a criminal organization exactly the same thing, the big guy. Strange isn't it?"

Just then Captain Hayes came into the room with two officers and the Captain said, "Armand, these officers will take you to the safe house and we will see if we can get your clothes and personal things from your apartment tomorrow morning and bring them to you."

"Just one more thing, I need you to leave your cell phone with me, since people can track your location using your cell phone. You will have a phone in the house that you will be able to stay in contact your folks and Thelma. However, to begin with, you will have limited use of the phone, but you will be able to call your mother and Thelma, but you can't call them tonight. OK?"

Armand handed his cell phone to Captain Hayes and said, "Do you think this is really necessary?"

"I'm sorry, but I do. We had one person several years ago we were looking out for and he kept calling people on his cell phone about the people he was providing information on. They tracked him down and almost killed him. Our people had to kill them to keep him alive. Since then, we don't allow people in our protective custody to have their personal cell phones."

"OK, thanks. I understand."

Then two officers came into the room and told Armand they were ready to take him to a safe house.

He got up and went with the officers with his head down, thinking what a fool he was to think the men he was working with were using him to get information to harm his friends in London.

CHAPTER TWENTY-FIVE

THE NOOSE IS GETTING TIGHTER

om told Captain Hayes what Armand told him about the department heads at the Finland Embassy. They fit with what the information they had from Charlie Wilson of the five men that headed up the drug dealers organization.

Captain Hayes said he now had Scotland Yard's investigators watching all of the locations that Charlie took them to. They would be watching every day and night to see what was going on in these locations and then on Friday to see if what Charlie told them was true. That he stopped to pick up money. It took a long time before Charlie finally realized they were picking up money for selling illegal drugs.

The Scotland Yard's investigators found as they watched these locations that on Friday a man in an Embassy Vehicle stopped at the location and came out with a bag which looked to be a bank bag. Then, on Saturday that same man came back to each of these locations and brought in two or three boxes that he took out of a large black Range Rover. The Range Rover had very dark tinted windows and had Embassy license plates on it.

The Captain said, "Tom, you know we can't search their Embassy for these drugs without their permission. Going into an Embassy is like entering their country without their permission and you know by the time we would get permission there wouldn't be any drugs in there."

That's a real problem Captain, but I might be able to help you out with that by instead of going into the Embassy we have the officials from Finland do it for us."

"I don't know how that could happen and I don't want to know. You understand that don't you?"

Tom said, "First, you have to understand my idea."

"OK."

"You know, Captain Hayes, these guys have a real sweet deal going on here. They bring everything into the country using diplomatic pouches or boxes that no one can search when it arrives in the country."

"I'm sure they must get several boxes every week for the number of locations they are servicing. The money must be piling up. So they must take the money out the same way, by probably sending it to a bank in Switzerland or having one of their men take it there."

The Captain said, "I think the only thing we can do is to shut down all of their sellers, but then they would just set up new locations, but at least it would disrupt their operation for a while."

"Captain, I have another idea of how to shut down their operation. What if I provided the information to the American Ambassador to Finland and he sets up a meeting and presented it to the head of Finland's Government."

"From what I know about Finland, these folks will be dealt with more harshly than anything the British Government could ever do to them."

"Good idea, Tom. I'll have our people take pictures of the guy delivering the drugs and picking up the money and pictures of the man taking boxes of drugs out of the Embassy vehicle."

"Plus, we will raid every location where the drugs are being sold on the same day and time, plus, we alert the TV Stations and the newspapers of the raids. So we get plenty of press about these raids."

Tom said, "I will ask the United States Ambassador to be there to let the leaders of Finland know about these raids. However, only just before they happen, but not too much before then, so they can't stop the guy from being arrested, as he is delivering the drugs and taking the boxes out of the Embassy vehicle."

Captain Hayes said "Our other problem is going to be able to prove that all five of the top officials at the Embassy are involved in the drug business."

"That's true, but maybe that won't make any difference to the head of Finland's government. If the other heads of the Embassy didn't know what was going on, why didn't they?"

"OK, its next Saturday when the raids are on at all locations where they are selling drugs brought from the men from the Finland Embassy."

The following Saturday, the America Ambassador was just starting his informal meeting with the head of Finland's government to advise him that Scotland Yard officers were making raids on several locations that were selling illegal drugs supplied by men from Finland's Embassy in London.

He gave them pictures of the boxes of drugs being taken out of the Embassy vehicle and pictures of the boxes of drugs being loaded into the vehicle from London's Finland Embassy. Included in the pictures when the boxes of drugs were being loaded into the vehicle was a picture of the London's Finnish Ambassador who was actually filmed handing the boxes to one of the Embassy employees inside the vehicle.

Soon after that, the local TV networks in Finland picked up on the story and a clerk came rushing in to the Head of Finland's government to alert him about the breaking news.

Hearing that news, the head of Finland's government sent a special Army Police Unit to London to bring back the top officers in charge of the London Embassy ASAP.

The next thing that happened on the streets of London was to see officers of Scotland Yard, surrounding the sidewalks around Finland's Embassy to be sure that no drugs were being removed from the building and the Land Rover with the dark tinted windows that had been parked on the city street had now been towed to the Scotland Yard Complex.

When the Finnish Army Police Unit arrived in London, they went directly to the Embassy and arrested Ambassador Zig Klebe and three of the other top officials of Finland's Embassy.

One man was missing, the one Tom called Evert, the terminator. He wasn't at the Embassy. Tom knew he was the one that if the gang couldn't find a way to work with someone he eliminated them, or another way of saying it, he just killed them.

The next thing the Finnish Army Police did was to form a line of men from inside the Embassy and they began passing the boxes of illegal drugs out to the sidewalk for the officers of Scotland Yards to haul away all of the drugs left in the Embassy.

The TV stations were having a field day watching and filming the Finnish Army Police passing box after box of drugs out of the Embassy to the sidewalk where the Scotland Yard officers were stacking the boxes up waiting for vehicles to haul them back to the Scotland Yard Complex.

When Evert heard the news about the top officials of Finland Embassy being taken into custody by the Finnish Army Police, he knew he couldn't go back to Finland. So, he would be leaving for South America, but before he left, he knew Tom Parker was behind all of this and he was determined to kill him before he left.

So, he called Tom's phone and when Tom answered, the man said, "Hello one more time, Tom Parker. This is Uranus Al ص Sadr and I'm leaving London, but before I do. I just have to kill you."

Then, he said you will be as dead as this phone will be."

He ended the call and Tom's phone was, indeed, dead.

Tom was now ready for Evert, the Terminator. He just didn't have any idea where he might try to kill him. One thing Tom knew he wanted to do was to be sure it wasn't anywhere around Jenny when Evert tried.

Tom had Benny come and pick him up in the Rolls and drive him toward the Scotland Yard complex, but before they had traveled only a few blocks Benny saw a small black car following them and he told Tom that he was sure that it was the same kind of little black car that followed behind them before.

Tom told Benny, "Just keep driving toward the Scotland Yard complex but a few blocks before you get there, I want you to drive toward the river and when you get there, slow way down and see if the black car will pass us. If it does, stop as soon as you can and let me out.

Then turn the Rolls around and drive only a little way away from where you let me out and park.

Benny did as Tom said, he drove very slowly and when the little black car passed him he stopped the Rolls. Tom got out of the car with his automatic weapon at the ready. The little black car turned around and headed back toward the Rolls and when he got behind the Rolls the driver stopped his car and got out.

Tom was waiting on the other side of the street where he had been hiding behind a small truck.

The Terminator got out of the black car and started making his way toward the Rolls, but Tom called out to the man, "Hey, are you looking for me Mr. Terminator? I'm over here."

The Terminator turned toward Tom with his pistol in his hand and Tom pulled the trigger on his automatic three times and down the Terminator went.

Tom walked over to where the Terminator's body lay and turned his body over to be sure he was dead and calmly said, "Terminator, you've been terminated."

Tom got into the Rolls and called Captain Hayes and when he answered the call. Tom said, "Captain Hayes, I just got the guy they called the Terminator, you can find his body laying on the sidewalk. Wait, I'll have my driver Benny tell you where we're at and we will be waiting for you here."

Tom handed his phone to Benny and Benny gave Captain Hayes the address to where the body was located."

Tom said, "Benny, tell him we will be waiting for him here."

Benny did.

CHAPTER TWENTY-SIX

IT'S TIME TO SAY GOODBYE TO ENGLAND AND GO HOME

Tom said, "Jenny, I think it's time to go home. I believe we have found out that the British Prime Minster Blake Pearson is not selling out America to help Russia in any way."

"In addition, Jenny, you've bought a couple of new Rolls Royce's and hired a European Manager to set up a new European Branch for your company, with its headquarters in the new DP World London Gateway complex."

Jenny replied, "Yes, and you have hired us a new driver to drive us in LA and it will also be your job to tell Robert Fong that he's too old to drive us around LA anymore."

Tom said, "Right, my love. I'll be sure to tell him right after Robert drives us home to our Beverly Hills home."

Then Tom said, "Don't you think it would be better if you told Robert, that you realized he had too much work to do by being the Butler and driving us all the time."

"After all, Robert is your Butler and is in charge of running your home, but then having him driving all of us around all the time is just too much to ask of him."

"So, after you met Benny you thought he could be a big help to Robert if you hired him to be you're driver. Plus, now that we're having two more people living with us all the time, it's even more work for him."

"My brave husband, you would rather take on twenty armed gunmen than tell Robert he's wasn't going to be both the Butler and our Chauffeur anymore."

"That's right if I killed them, I wouldn't have to feel bad if one of them was crying about not getting to live one more day."

Tom remembered that he promised to let Blake Pearson know when they were leaving to go back to the USA. So, Tom called him and Blake asked him to not leave London before he had a chance to talk with him.

Blake said, "I know there is no way you would leave without talking with your almost best friend in the whole world."

Tom replied, "You're right, so would it be all right if you could come to the airport to see me off?"

"Certainly, I'll be there as soon as I can get there."

"We wouldn't leave until you get here."

Jenny asked, "Tom, what did Blake Pearson say about you leaving London?"

"He just said that he had to come to see us off, since I'm his almost best friend and I should never leave without seeing him and telling him good bye."

"So, I told him he was right. He said he would come out and see us before we left and that he needed to tell his almost best friend good bye."

About thirty minutes passed before Blake and Suri arrived, and by that time, Jenny was already in the plane while Tom waited in the limo. Tom got out of the limo and met Blake and Suri, Suri gave Tom a hug and a kiss and then went into the plane to wish Jenny good bye and to thank her again for saving them from the kidnappers.

Blake asked Tom to get into his limo and for the driver to wait outside the car while he talked to Tom.

Blake said, "Tom, my almost best friend, I have to tell you that I'm very sorry for all of the problems you've had since you been in London and I'm afraid it all my fault."

"I don't know how it could be your fault, it was the guys from the drug dealers that somehow thought I was in London to help investigate them."

Blake said, "Well, they probably thought that because they had something that they could used on me due to a big mistake I made when I went on a trip with Peter Valkovich without Suri. We went to see about some new products he was thinking about trying to sell that was made in Finland."

"Anyway, he was meeting with these people and I went to my room and a very pretty young woman knocked on my hotel door and when I answered the door she just came into my room. She had a bottle of Champagne in her hand and said, "I came to give you a nightcap it's part of the service from the hotel."

"She poured me a glass-full and a glass for herself, and I drank my glass-full and began to feel like I was going to fall down, so I sat down on the bed and passed out."

"I don't remember anything after that."

"The next morning when I woke up, I had a stack of pictures that they left for me and this young woman was in bed with me and a lot of other explicit pictures indicating I was in various sexual positions with this girl."

"I was told these pictures would be sent to Suri and the London Times if I didn't turn a blind eye to their drug business and the Russian efforts in Europe."

"I'm sorry to say I did both, and I'm so thrilled you got involved and took out the drug dealers and the Russian threat in Europe without the UK standing up to them."

"So, my almost best friend I have to thank you for taking out these drug dealers and freeing me so I can do my job for the United Kingdom and Europe."

Also, you gave me the courage to finally tell Suri what had happened to me."

"Blake, do you think Peter had any part of this?"

"No, I don't so. I think that these people saw pictures of me meeting with some of the people that Peter was meeting and the newspaper article told everyone where I was staying."

"Well, my almost best friend Blake, I appreciate you telling me about all of this and I'm sorry these people caught you in a trap to be able to help them with their drug business. One of the reasons, well, actually the real reason that Jenny and I were here was to find out if you had gone to the Russian side and I can report to the President that you haven't."

Blake said, "You can assure your President that I am not on the Russian side."

Blake, my almost best friend, I will do that and he will be pleased to hear it."

Tom and Blake got out of the limo and walked over to the waiting jet that was ready to take off for the United States.

Both Suri and Jenny came out of the plane and Suri said, "Well, I hope my husband and his almost best friend got everything squared away between England and America."

Tom put on his best smile and replied, "You can be sure he did."

Tom gave Suri a kiss and told her to come to Hollywood and see us.

Blake also gave Jenny a big kiss and Jenny said, "Thank you for being Toms almost best friend, and please take care of yourself and don't be traveling without Suri by your side."

Now Blake was sure that Suri had told Jenny exactly what he had told Tom.

After having hugs all around, Tom and Jenny boarded their plane and Blake and Suri got into their limo and all were now on their way home.

When they arrived in LA, Robert was waiting with the limo to pick them up. As soon as they all cleared customs and immigration. Tom introduced Benny Johnson to Robert Fong. Then the two of them started talking as they were carrying the luggage over to the trunk. At the same time Tom was making arrangements to have the rest of their luggage delivered to their home.

Benny opened the door for Jenny to get into the car as Tom was getting in on the other side of the car. Then, Robert got into the driver's seat and Benny got in beside him.

As Robert drove them home, Benny and Robert were having a long conversation in the front seat and when they arrived at their home, Robert and Benny got out of the limo and Robert opened Jenny's door and Benny opened Tom's door.

When Jenny was out of the limo, Robert said, "Miss Jenny, thank you for hiring Benny to be your driver. It will certainly take a lot of work off of me. I like him a lot and I think he will fit into the family just fine."

Jenny just smiled and said, "Thank you, Robert, it is really good to be home and I hope we can make it all the way into the house without someone trying to kill us."

Just then Jenny heard a lot of popping noise. She looked at Tom, then she heard Robert say, "It's the fourth of July, so there's lots of fireworks going off tonight."

Tom took Jenny's hand and said, "Happy fourth, my love."

THE END